THE Boy PROBLEM

(Notes and Predictions of Tabitha Reddy)

Also by Kami Kinard

The Boy Project (Notes and Observations of Kara McAllister)

THE Boy PROBLEM

(Notes and Predictions of Tabitha Reddy)

KAMI KINARD

Scholastic Press
New York

Library of Congress Cataloging-in-Publication Data Available

ISBN 978-0-545-57586-7

12 11 10 9 8 7 6 5 4 3 2 1   14 15 16 17 18/0

Printed in the U.S.A.

First printing, January 2014

Book design by Whitney Lyle

Illustrations © Kami Kinard

For my parents, who never let me run out of books

Friday, August 31
My room / 8:30 p.m.

Most people don't think it's possible to predict the future. I'm one of the exceptions.

I believe in signs — little clues that hint at things that might happen someday. You just have to be open to seeing them.

My BFF, Kara McAllister, doesn't think like I do. She's what you'd call a cynic. I mean, a sign can be *right in front* of her face, pointing her down the road to future events, but she'd rather figure out a way to explain why it *isn't* a sign at all than go ahead and believe that it *is* one.

Earlier tonight a VERY OBVIOUS sign landed right under my nose. Literally. I know that it means something FANTASTIC is going to happen to me this year! But did Kara interpret it the way I did? Well . . . I'm not exactly sure.

We'd gone to Triple Slice Pizza with Kara's boyfriend, Chip, to celebrate the last Friday before the start of the new school year. Kara and Chip sat on one side of the booth. I sat on the other. Alone.

So even though they PROMISED that I wasn't one, I pretty much felt like a third wheel before we even placed our order. You don't have to be a math genius (and trust me, I'm not) to figure out these two equations:

$$2 + 1 = \text{Third Wheel}$$
$$3 - 1 = \text{Date}$$

DUH!

That's one reason why I was more than happy to leave them by themselves when the cute guy at the window shouted: "Order up for McAllister!"

Actually, I had some other reasons for volunteering to get the pizza. (See above sentence. There was a CUTE GUY at the window!) More importantly, I wanted a chance to spy on Colleen McCarver, the *wickedest, sickest* girl at our school. (Just to be clear, I mean *wicked* and *sick* in a bad way . . . although now that I think about it, she's so popular that most people probably think she's wicked and sick in a cool way. Whatever!) Not that I cared what she was doing, because I totally didn't, but I did care about who she was with:

See, last year Alex dumped Maybelline for a *high school* cheerleader. (FYI: Kara and I call Colleen McCarver *Maybelline* because she wears so much makeup.) Anyway, that breakup was the gossip of the millennium at Spring Valley Middle. I'm not even joking.

I didn't see how Maybelline could possibly take Alex back after he'd publicly humiliated her like that, even if he is superstar gorgeous. I know *I* wouldn't give him another chance. No way!

(Still . . . Alex B didn't break up with *me* for a cheerleader. So if he was suddenly available . . .)

I glanced their way as I walked by their booth. Alex B was concentrating on opening a pack of crackers. That was a good sign! (For me, not Maybelline.) I mean, it's kind of OVER when your crush is more interested in a pack of crackers than in you!

Crackers > Crush = Doomed Relationship

Our order was waiting a few steps away. I picked up the pizza and inhaled. I'm CRAZY for the smell of fresh pizza dough — or any kind of dough, really. Mom used to bake all the time before Dad left. Not just pizza, but breads, cakes, and cookies, too. I soooo miss that smell.

Flour + Butter + Mixer + Oven = Nose Paradise

That's the smell, when I think about it, of a happy home.

I looked over at Alex and Maybelline again as I walked back to our booth. No eye or body contact between them! ☺

When I reached our table with the extra-large triple-cheese pizza, Kara and Chip quickly slid apart. That wasn't AWKWARD for me or anything. Geez!

"I can't tell if they're back together or not," I reported, "but at least Maybelline doesn't look like a third wheel."

"You're NOT a third wheel," said Kara, who was holding hands with Chip under the table.

"Yes, I am," I said. "And it looks like I'm going to be one forever. I'll never find the right guy!" I believed it, too, because I have a boy problem. I've been super-unlucky in love. Look at the two guys I dated last year.

1. Evan Carlson
2. James Powalski

At first, I thought both guys were AWESOME. Boy, was I WRONG.

Wrong + Wrong ≠ Mr. Right

See the problem? Anyway, I was about to put the pizza down on the table when Kara looked over my shoulder and said, "Hey, an *absolutely adorable* guy just walked in who totally looks like a third wheel! Let's invite him to sit with you!"

I looked over my shoulder. I shouldn't have.

For one thing, it was just a kindergartner with his mom and dad. Very funny, Kara. For another, it turns out that carrying an extra-large triple-cheese pizza requires full concentration, and in the moment that I turned my head, I felt the tray slipping from my grip. I dug my thumbs into the piping-hot crust to try to keep the pizza from falling.

Why is it that when you sink your teeth into hot pizza dough you're like, "Mmmmm," but when you sink your thumbs into it you're like, "YEEEOOOOWWWWWWWW!"

Right then I had a slo-mo mo. (Slow-motion moment. You know, one of those moments that only takes, like, five seconds, but because the five seconds are so MORTIFYING, they seem to drag on for an ETERNITY.)

Believe it or not, I managed to hold on to the pizza. Well, most of it. The crust was saved! But the triple cheese slid into an asymmetrical pile on the red-and-white-tiled floor.

"Tabbi!" cried Chip and Kara at the exact same time.

I was too mesmerized to say *jinx*, though. I just stood there, staring at the ruined cheese. Then I realized I was witnessing something *more* than just a pile of cheese. Something unbelievable. Something amazing. A sign!

I slammed the tray down on the table and whipped out my cell phone. In less than thirty seconds, I had eight photos of the cheesy floor.

"What are you *doing*?" asked Kara.

I pointed to the cheese. "Don't you see? It looks *exactly* like a guy's head!"

"Not to me," said Kara.

"That's because you're looking at it upside down. Come over here."

Kara slid out of the booth and stood next to me.

Chip grabbed the pizza tray. "I'm gonna see if they'll throw more cheese on this pie. And if they will . . ." He looked directly at me. "You're eating the pieces with the thumb holes in the crust."

"Oh. Well." I turned back to the cheese and pointed. "See, Kara, that's the ear. And that lump there is the nose."

"Hmmm," said Kara in a way that made clear she wasn't seeing what I was.

"And this is his hairline." I pointed to a jagged edge that jutted out from the gooey forehead. "Don't you think it looks exactly like a guy?"

"I guess I can kind of see it," said Kara.

"Kind of see it? I'll tell you what I see: the image of my future crush. Look at that handsome profile! He's perfect for me!"

I was *not* backing down until Kara admitted she saw cheese guy. Tabbi Reddy never gives up, and she never backs down!

Kara squinched up her face and tilted her head.

About then a waitress came over with a trash can and a dustpan. She started to kneel next to the cheese head.

"Wait!" I cried. I pointed to a crack in the cheese that was CLEARLY an eye. "Here's the eye. *Now* can you see him?"

Kara looked like she was concentrating. "Yes! I see him! I really do!" She seemed to mean it. She turned to the waitress and said, "Look! See how that cheese is shaped like a guy's head?"

"I just see someone else's mess that I have to clean up," the waitress said. "And two crazy girls." She scooped up the cheese head in a single swoop and dumped him into the trash can.

Some people have no vision.

Kara and I slid back into the booth. I excitedly scrolled through the cheese pics on my cell. "This is the best day of my life!" I said.

"You're either overreacting," said Kara, "or losing it."

"Am not! That pile of cheese was a sign — a sign from the universe that the right guy is out there for me after all!"

"Or maybe it was only a pile of cheese," said Kara.

I scowled.

"That looked remarkably like a head," she added quickly.

"Think about it," I said. "One tiny MILLISEC after I said *I'll never find the right guy*, the universe tipped my hands forward and the cheese slid off of the pizza and landed in the *exact* shape of a guy's head. Maybe even the *right* guy's head!" I waved the picture on my phone in front of her face.

Kara looked skeptical. "Or . . . it's possible that the pizza fell because you were distracted . . . or clumsy."

"No," I said. "No way. I've carried pizza trays from that window to these tables tons of times and I've never dropped so much as a pepperoni. I'm telling you. It's a sign that predicts the future Mr. Right!"

Before Kara could comment, Chip interrupted. He plopped the pizza with its new single layer of cheese down on the table. "I'm starved. Let's eat!"

I glanced up at him and saw Maybelline and Alex B leaving. She was showing him something on her cell phone and laughing hysterically. He had his arm around her shoulders. I guess they were back together after all. ☹!

Amazing how an entire year can go by and nothing changes. Maybelline is starting off the school year with Alex B. And once again, I am starting off the school year with no one. The only thing that has really changed is Kara's boyfriend status.

Oh. Well. It's hard to be bummed about anything now that I've gotten a positive sign from the universe. And I think if I look closely enough, I'll find more signs. It doesn't matter if Kara agrees with me or not. When it comes to the future, I like to make my own predictions.

My prediction: The right guy is out there waiting for me to find him.

Sunday, September 2
My room / 10:30 a.m.

Kara's mom said that I could sleep over last night. I LOVE staying at Kara's house because her reasonable mom lets us stay up late and talk, unlike my obsessive mom, who is waaaaaaay strict about bedtime. Actually, my mom is kinda waaaaaaay strict about everything. She claims it helps her feel like she's in control of her life, which she says went out of control when my dad left. Ha! That's just an excuse for her being the way she's always been: the strictest mom on the planet!

Anyway, last night Kara and I were lying on her bedroom floor, looking at the glow-in-the-dark stars on her ceiling.

Me: Wouldn't it be great if these were all make-a-wish stars?

Kara: I guess.

Me: *You guess?* It'd totally ROCK!

Kara: Tabs, please tell me you know wishes don't all come true, even if you make them on stars.

Me: Wishing on a star just *has* to give your wish a better chance of coming true!

In my mind, it was simple math.

Wish + ★ > Wish − ★

Kara: *Nothing* helps your wishes come true unless YOU do something yourself. It's called being *proactive*, Tabs.

Kara's big on that word. *Proactive.* But I think there are lots of things we can't POSSIBLY control. So I figure wishing on stars and paying attention to where signs point can only help.

I focused on a cluster of stars over Kara's desk. If I could make any wish, I'd want my dad to come back home. But that's not going to happen and I know it. He already has a new family. And if I made that wish, then some other kid, my little half brother, Toby, would be without a dad.

I let my eyes wander around the ceiling until they landed on one tiny star, stuck in a corner above Kara's closet door. I wonder if she meant to leave it there all by itself.

I closed my eyes and silently wished I'd find that guy — the one whose face was in that pizza cheese. Kara interrupted my thoughts.

Kara: So how are you going to be proactive?

Me: I don't know. I'm not like you, Kara. I can't just come up with a project and, *whammo*, suddenly I have the perfect boyfriend.

Kara (sitting up): Hey! That project was a lot of work! And I didn't find Chip suddenly. It took *months*! I didn't even like him at first . . . but later I saw his potential.

That got me thinking that maybe the right guy for me is someone like Chip, who I already know. Maybe I just haven't seen his potential yet. When I told Kara this she got up and grabbed one of her notebooks. We made a list of eligible guys in our class:

Boys Who Might Have Hidden Potential

1. Evan
2. James
3. Phillip
4. Chip
5. Alex B
6. Alex L
7. Malcolm
8. Jonah Nate
9. Malik
10. Richie
11. Gil
12. Dylan
13. T.J.
14. Jake
15. Josh
16. Collin

But even as I was putting the list down on paper, I could see why none of these guys would work out.

Boys Who Might Have Hidden Potential- NOT

#	Name	Reason
1.	Evan	He's had his chance
2.	James	Ditto
3.	Phillip	Taken
4.	Chip	Taken
5.	Alex B	Taken (drat!)
6.	Alex L	Taken forever (who cares!)
7.	Malcolm	Too weird
8.	Jonah Nate	Too dorky
9.	Malik	Don't know him
10.	Richie	Too quiet
11.	Gil	Too short
12.	Dylan	Snob
13.	T.J.	Had too many GFs
14.	Jake	Taken
15.	Josh	Not interested
16.	Collin	Too nerdy

So in the end, my list pretty much looked like this:

If there's hidden potential in any of the guys in my class, it's gonna take a CIA investigator to find it.

Kara tried to cheer me up by pointing out that the first

day of school is this coming Monday. DUH! I've had all my new, super-cute school supplies, including this journal (I buy one at the start of every school year), for about a week. I can't help it! I get really excited about the first day of a school year because each new year has so much potential. (Even if none of the *guys* have it.)

Speaking of potential, that was Kara's whole point: Every year there are a few new guys in our classes who've transferred in from other schools.

I thought about the potential of a new year with new boys, and I went to sleep with a bit of hope glowing inside me like that tiny little star randomly stuck over Kara's closet door.

Monday, September 3
My room / 7:01 a.m.

Yesterday I was feeling hopeful, but this morning, reality hit as soon as my feet touched the orange shag rug on my bedroom floor. I'm completely freaking out! About a million questions are invading my brain.

What if the pizza head sign really was just a lump of cheese? What if wishing on stars means your wishes NEVER come true? What if I can't understand algebra? What if I think my white skinny jeans, aqua tank, and beaded flats make a super-cute outfit, but really it's the definition of stupid?

AND today will be the first time I've seen James since I broke his ♥ by breaking up with him. I mean, he *begged* for us to stay together. What if he can't resist me when he sees me again? AWKWARD!

And where will I sit at lunch? With Kara and Chip? Will I be a third wheel FOR THE REST OF THE YEAR?

This queasy, heart-racing feeling reminds me of how I felt last year on the day I had to go back to school after cutting off all of my long blond hair.

FYI: I didn't INTEND to cut my hair off, it just kind of happened. I mean, when I decided to take a relaxing bath in our new jet tub, how could I possibly know I'd end up with THE WORLD'S LARGEST TANGLE?!!!!

It's not like anyone was around to tell me to put my hair up before turning on the jets! You've heard of a tangle being called a rat's nest, right? Well, my hair was like a rat's condominium or something. It had nest on top of nest on top of nest on top of nest.

Condo for Rats
Units Available

At first, Mom tried to help me untangle it the old-fashioned way: with a brush and comb. After about an hour of torturous tugging, the situation was still so hopeless that she gave up and resorted to going online to look for suggestions.

She came back into the bathroom with a jar of peanut butter. She spread it all over my hair, like I was a slice of bread waiting to be turned into a record-breaking PB&J sandwich. Then she tried to unravel the giant knot again.

No luck!

"Wait right here!" she said, as if I'd go anywhere sporting a peanut butter–coated do. I mean, one whiff of my head, and the squirrels in our yard would go NUTZ. Literally.

Things were not looking up when Mom came back into the bathroom.

Yep, she really was carrying olive oil, mayonnaise, and a banana.

Before she could turn my head into a fruit salad, I told her I'd just remembered a foolproof way to remove tangles.

Then I grabbed a pair of scissors from the counter and started hacking off my hair.

Mom actually screamed. You'd think I used those scissors to stab her with or something.

When I was finished, my formerly beautiful hair lay like a dead animal on the tile floor. I hate to say it, but after the jet tub and peanut butter treatment, it looked so disgusting that it was hard to believe that mess was ever attached to my head.

While Mom ate the banana (turns out she wasn't going to put it in my hair — she'd just worked up an appetite trying to get my tangles out), I took a loooooonnnnnnngggggg shower to get the nutty smell out of my new short hair.

My mane still looked pretty scary even after I washed and dried it! And I still smelled like an appetizer for an elephant.

Seriously, I may never eat a Reese's cup again.

But the next day Mom took me to Fabien's Divine Hair so Fabien could "work his magic." (His magic includes keeping Mom blond, BTW.)

Fabien ooohed and ahhhed over my butchered hair, calling it thick and glossy. (Saying stuff like that probably works like an imaginary hand — reaching out to collect bigger tips!)

"Honey, this child is sooooo luuuuuuCKY!" He told my mom as he scissor-sculpted my hair. "Not many girls her age have a face cute enough to pull off a pixie."

When Fabien was finished snipping, even *I* had to admit that he was a hair magician. But after that, I went home and sat in front of the mirror for, like, two hours. Despite the fact that my short hair looked fab, I was totally freaked out about seeing my friends (and my enemies) at school the next morning.

I decided the best thing to do was to face the day with confidence and act like I'd cut my hair off because I *wanted* it that way.

And now that I'm writing about it, I have to admit everything turned out okay. I ended up liking my short hair so much that I never went back to long hair. So that jet tub accident must have been a sign — signaling me to change my hairstyle.

Whew. I feel a lot better now. I just need to face the new school year with confidence! If I never meet the guy I saw in the pizza cheese, I can always take James back. He'll jump at the chance, and at least I won't have to be an everlasting third wheel.

Man, does it feel good to have a PLAN B!

Family room / 3:33 p.m.

On a scale of one to ten, I give today a four. Not that today was all bad — it wasn't. It's just that I found out something unbelievably horrible this morning, and the horrible thing is winning the tug-of-war against the good things.

One Unbelievably Horrible Thing > Lots of Good Things

Let me get the horrible stuff over with. James has a new girlfriend! She's one of two new girls in our grade: Kaitlin. The prettier one! She looks like she's cool, too, in the soon-to-be-popular way. Man, I thought *he'd* be the one feeling awkward, since he seemed so upset when I broke up with him, but NOPE! I get to keep that awkward feeling all to myself. Seeing him and Kaitlin look so happy together made me wonder why I broke up with him. I mean . . . if he's good enough for her . . .

Oh well. So much for Plan B.

What really stinks is that I can't even avoid James, because he's in my algebra class. Unfortunately, so is Priyanka Gupta. Ugh.

I noticed Priyanka as soon as I stepped through the doorway. She immediately began waving madly at me from across the room. She was wearing lime-green knee socks with cupcakes printed on them, a pink T-shirt that said *Keep Calm and Eat a Cupcake*, and she had a cupcake pencil topper on her pink pencil.

Physically, Priyanka's a tiny person, about two inches shorter than me, and I'm not tall. But even though she's tiny, everything about her is big. She has a big voice — loud, like her clothes! Her hair is extremely long and very black. Her smile seems too big for her face. Her large brown-black eyes have ridiculously long eyelashes that are the secret envy of every girl at Spring Valley Middle. When she talks, she makes sweeping movements with her arms — as in, you have to stand about three feet back from her to keep from being hit by the sweeping! One thing about her is obvious: Priyanka Gupta isn't going to let her small size keep her from being noticed.

I don't know why, but Priyanka's enthusiasm for everything kind of annoys me, so I gave her a quick wave back and took a seat near the doorway, which was as far away from her as I could sit. It's not like I really know Priyanka that well or anything. Still, I kind of *had* to wave back, but I didn't *have* to sit by her.

Unfortunately I'd been so busy trying to avoid Priyanka that the seat I took was smack in front of James. My butt had hardly hit the chair when he said, "Couldn't stay away, could you, Tabbi? Too bad for you. I'm taken."

I turned around and gave him my signature *couldn't care*

less glare. "Yeah, I know. I wish she'd *take* you to *another country.*"

That seemed to shut him up, so I settled back into my chair and waited for the torture to begin. Since schools can't offer classes in torture, they give this painful experience the name *algebra* to try to fool unsuspecting students.

But things turned out not to be so torturous after all.

I'd been dreading algebra because Kara told me Mr. DeLacey, the algebra teacher, was a real jerk. But apparently, Mr. D has left the school! So we have a new teacher.

His name is Mr. Gheary. He is tall and skinny and seems to embrace his nerdiness. Here's how I'd sum him up:

$$\text{Black-framed Glasses + Teaching Degree} = \text{Nerdy and I Know It}$$

Mr. Gheary stood in front of the class with his hands in his pockets and said, "Class." Then he waited. "Class," he said again, a little louder. We got quiet, but Mr. Gheary still looked at us without saying anything. I guess he's big on the dramatic pause. You know, getting everyone's attention, then NOT talking.

Still not talking, Mr. G pulled a quarter out of his pocket and started flipping it. He did this over and over, each time catching it in his right hand, then slapping it down on the back of his left. He called out *heads* or *tails* after each flip.

I didn't know what the man was thinking — like we didn't have anything better to do than watch him flip a coin! Okay: I really *didn't* have anything better to do than to watch him flip a coin! Because if I weren't doing that, I'd probably be stuck doing algebra problems from the book or something.

After he flipped Washington's head about a zillion times, he said, "Each time I flip this coin, there are two possible outcomes."

"Heads or tails!" shouted Priyanka, throwing her arms in the air excitedly.

Mr. G gave a quick nod in her direction, as if the rest of us couldn't have come up with this very obvious answer.

"Did anyone notice how many times I said *heads*, versus how many times I said *tails*?" he asked.

There was a pause, but not a dramatic pause. More like a *someone else please answer before he calls on me* pause.

Luckily, Mr. G continued. "Can anyone guess, then, whether the amount of times the coin landed on heads was greater than, less than, or equal to the number of times it landed on tails?"

"Equal to!" shouted Priyanka, almost jumping out of her seat. Mr. G gave her a little smile this time. "Correct," he said. Priyanka's huge smile threatened to take over her entire face. Then Mr. G added, "In theory." Good-bye, huge smile. See ya!

Mr. Gheary went on to explain that because there are only two sides to the coin, the *probability* of a coin landing on heads is equal to its landing on tails. But that doesn't mean it happens that way every time, in practice.

To prove this, he handed out coins and told us to pick a partner. I grabbed LaTisha Jeffers before anyone worse could grab me. Our assignment was to flip the coin a hundred times and record whether it landed on heads or tails. In the end, our tally sheet looked like this:

Heads	Tails
卌 卌 卌	卌 卌
卌 卌	卌 卌
卌 卌	卌
卌 卌	|
卌 卌	
卌 卌	
卌 |||	

It was soooooo NOT fifty-fifty! But then Mr. G had all of the teams come up and write their totals on the board. There were twelve pairs of us, so that's one thousand two hundred coin flips. When you added everyone's totals together, it was a *lot closer* to a fifty-fifty split.

Mr. G explained that probability isn't so reliable in predicting an individual flip, but it can predict the expected results for a large number of flips.

Before I knew it, the bell was ringing. How did algebra go by so fast?

GTG! I was supposed to be at Kara's house ten minutes ago!

My room / 6:17 p.m.

Every year, Kara and I compare first-day-of-school report cards, where we rank our teachers and predict how we're going to like our classes. Mine looks like this:

Period/ Subject	Teacher	Prediction
1/ English	Hill	Oh no! Why'd she have to change grades? No need to predict what English will be like. We already know you can't get away with anything in *her* class!
2/ Humanities	Martinez	She loves ancient civilizations. LOVES them. I'm pretty sure she started drooling a little when talking about the Egyptians. This may excite Ms. Martinez, but I predict this class will be a snoozer!
3/ Algebra	Gheary	Maybe less awful than I predicted.
4/ Science	Pederson	Not bad. We did an experiment with candy bars today. Cool points for any teacher who lets us eat Snickers in class on day one. Hopefully tomorrow's experiment will involve Skittles!
5/ Lunch		Best period of the day! Even if I was a third wheel in the cafeteria.
6/ Advisory	Ries	AKA free reading, or study hall, except on days we have discussion groups!
7/ (A day) Health	Smith	Let's face it, no one likes talking about basic bodily functions and infectious diseases.
7/ (B day) Band	Waldorf	Can you say *automatic A?* I predict this class will rock, once again.

Kara's report card, though, was 100 percent positive. She thinks every class is going to be interesting and every teacher is going to be nice. She's my BFF and all, but she was getting on my NERVES gushing about how great her day was.

Let's see . . . why does Kara's year look all

And my year look all

Oh yeah, because she has a boyfriend and I don't! School schedules just look better when you have a boyfriend.

My prediction: Her year isn't going to be as great as she thinks. Nobody's is!

My room / 9:00 p.m.

I didn't have anything better to do after dinner, so I took out the completely useless list of guys with boyfriend potential — in other words, the blank sheet of paper.

Truthfully, there *were* three new guys in my classes. But I'm not adding their names to the list. It's hard for me to imagine that any of them have potential when two are a foot shorter than I am and the other one carries a SpongeBob backpack. Come on!

When I was walking to first period, though, I actually saw a very cute guy with dark, curly hair. I was too far away to get a really good look at him, but it only took a glimpse to see that HE had potential! I hadn't seen him around last year, so I hoped he was a cute new transfer student who I'd soon get to know in one of my classes. But no. Before I got to English, I saw him turn onto the sixth grade hall. Too bad! He might have potential for *someone* (a sixth grader) but not for me!

Anyway, I started absentmindedly folding the useless list into a cootie catcher. You know, those little origami squares that some people call *fortune-tellers*. I made tons of those back in fourth grade, so it only took me fifteen seconds to create one.

I flicked my fingers back and forth, watching it open and close like the beak of a hungry baby bird. I wondered how many possible outcomes there are for a cootie catcher. When he was flipping that quarter today, Mr. G made a big point that there were only two possible outcomes. Heads or tails.

With a normal cootie catcher, all choices lead to the same four squares. So basically, it would have twice as many outcomes as flipping a coin.

But if you used *each section* of the cootie catcher to tell *part* of a fortune, instead of putting all of the information in the last four sections, there would be all kinds of·possible outcomes!

$$(4 \text{ Possibilities})^4 = 256 \text{ Different Possible Boys!}$$

That gave me an idea . . . a way to solve my boy problem . . . a way to be what Kara calls *proactive*.

I grabbed a pencil and created the best, the most amazing cootie catcher ever. One that was sure to CHANGE MY LIFE! Or at least change the rest of the school year. Here's what it looked like:

LOVE-PREDICTOR
Cootie Catcher

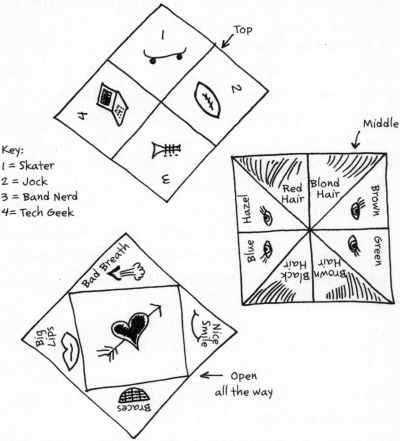

Key:
1 = Skater
2 = Jock
3 = Band Nerd
4 = Tech Geek

I, Tabitha Reddy, have invented the love-predictor cootie catcher!

I decided to be my own first customer, so I tried it out.

Cootie catcher prediction: An instrument-playing, brown-haired, green-eyed guy with a nice smile will like me.

I can't think of anyone who fits that description, but hey — there's always a chance someone new will show up for band tomorrow.

My prediction: Love success!

Tuesday, September 4
Mrs. Hill's room / 7:45 a.m.

I showed Kara my love-predictor cootie catcher before school and she totally dissed it! She says there's no way I can predict who my next crush will be using a "toy" that I made myself.

My prediction: Kara is wrong.

Family room / 4:17 p.m.

I can sum up most of the school day with this phrase: *Blah, blah, blah.*

Except for band. That's when things got exciting. At least for me.

Mr. Waldorf started us off with a piece from last year's spring concert to warm us up. I was pretty much able to play it from memory, which allowed my eyes to wander around the band room. I was looking for two things:

1. Brown hair
2. Green eyes

I'd worry about the nice smile later, since almost everyone's lips were too busy playing instruments to smile.

It didn't take me long to figure out that there was only one guy in the room who fit the love-predictor cootie catcher's prediction.

> 10 Guys with Brown Hair
> - 6 Guys with Brown Eyes
> - 3 Guys with Blue Eyes
> _____
> 1 Possibility

And I wasn't even sure about him because I HAD NO CLUE WHAT COLOR HIS EYES WERE!

Malcolm Maxwell has this cool longish hair. It's great, really. It makes him look like he belongs in a band — not the Spring Valley Middle School band, but the kind of band that makes the covers of magazines like *Astroteen* and *Drama Tween*. The only problem with his hair is that his long bangs cover his eyes. Trying to get a glimpse of them is like trying to see the rocks behind a waterfall.

Kara used to say there was something mysterious about Malcolm. Now I see what she means. But if Malcolm is a mystery, how do I crack the case? How can I get a view of his eyes?

A word that Kara uses WAY too much floated into my brain and drifted up to the top of my mind like a cube of ice in a glass of lemonade.

👍Proactive👍

If I wanted information, I needed to be a detective. When Mr. Waldorf stopped directing and started talking, I turned around and checked out my suspect again. He was looking down, which gave me a chance to notice that his eyelashes were very long. Nice.

He was absentmindedly twirling a drumstick in his right hand. *Very* nice. He didn't seem to be paying much attention to what Mr. Waldorf was saying. Normal.

Malcolm had grown taller over the summer, and his face was more angular. I watched him twirl that drumstick for a long time. He never looked up, so it was easy to watch him undetected.

Or so I thought.

Unfortunately, I *was* detected.

By Mr. Waldorf.

He called me out in front of the entire band! (I guess this doesn't say much for my detecting skills.)

"Tabbi Reddy, what's so interesting in the back of the room?" Mr. Waldorf yelled. Everyone in the class was suddenly looking at me.

In that same instant — BAM — so was Malcolm. The humiliation of being yelled at turned out to be worth it. Yep. Eye contact.

Then I wheeled around in my seat and looked apologetically at Mr. Waldorf, who did *not* look apologetically back at me, even though he'd just embarrassed me in front of the entire band! Rude!

I couldn't risk turning back around again, but my flute didn't play another note for the rest of the period. I just kinda held it in front of my lips and moved my fingers around. How could I be expected to produce music when all I could think about were those eyes? Those beautiful eyes that looked into mine for a millisecond before I turned around. Those eyes that can be described with one word: green.

Cootie catcher prediction: Malcolm Maxwell will be my next boyfriend.

My prediction: Band will be my favorite class!

My room / 8:15 p.m.

Just got off of the phone with Kara. Our conversation went something like this:

Me: The cootie catcher worked! It predicted who my next boyfriend will be. I mean, I haven't checked out his smile yet, but I'm sure it's great.

Kara: Wait — are you saying you have a new boyfriend?

Me: Not yet. But I know who it's gonna be.

Kara: Unless it's official, you never really know.

Me: Gah! Why do you have to be so logical about everything? Want to know who it is?

Kara: Sure.

Me (determined to be positive about this even though Kara's response wasn't exactly encouraging): Malcolm Maxwell.

Kara:

Me: Well. . . . say something.

Kara: Sorry. Just thinking.

Me: I guess that's better than your saying it will never work.

Kara: It'll never work.

Me: Gee. Thanks.

Kara: Well, I can see why you're interested. . . .

Me: He's cute, isn't he?

Kara: In a mysterious kind of way.

Me: I know, right?

Kara: But . . .

Me: What?

Kara: He's so . . . different. Like, how would you get a chance to talk to him? And even if you did find a chance, how would you get *him* to talk to *you*?"

I didn't know the answer to that one. You couldn't exactly *make* someone talk. I knew that. But I also knew something else. You could sure try.

My prediction: I'll be talking to Malcolm by the end of the week.

Wednesday, September 5
Kitchen / 7:01 a.m.

I refuse to think about Malcolm today, since I don't have band and it's unlikely that our paths will cross anyway.

Mrs. Hill's room / 7:40 a.m.

I can't stop thinking about Malcolm! How do you NOT think about the person you are destined to be with? The cootie catcher predicted it! If I see him at lunch or something I'm going to go up to him and see if I can get him to smile. Not that I need to prove that he has a nice smile. I'm sure he does.

Ms. Martinez's room / 8:43 a.m.

I can't go up to Malcolm and try to get him to talk. I can't! I will look obvious, desperate, or BOTH — thanks to Mr. Waldorf calling attention to the fact that I was staring at him. Oh, cootie catcher, why didn't you give me an easier target?

My room / 8:50 p.m.

Tomorrow will be the day. The day I find out if Malcolm is *the one*. I'm *determined* to talk to him.

I told this to Kara and she said, "Good luck. You know I observed him last year, and I only ever got to hear him say something like eighteen words. That's *all* year long."

I asked her if she'd ever really tried to talk to him. She had to admit that the longest "conversation" she'd ever had with him was when she was hiding out in a stall in the boys' room (long story), and she was trying NOT to talk to him at that point. So I don't think Kara's experience with Malcolm is a reliable prediction of what mine will be at all. I WILL talk to him until I catch a smile. I'm not backing down.

Kara's prediction: Malcolm won't talk.

My prediction: Yes, he will.

Thursday, September 6
My room / 3:10 p.m.

Oh. Yes. I. Did!

I walked right up to Malcolm and said, "You do an awesome job on the drums." (It sounds like a stupid thing to say now that I write it down, but trust me, it sounded better when I said it. I'm pretty sure it did, anyway.)

He said, "Thanks." But he didn't smile!

So I said, "I'm Tabbi, I'm in the flute section."

And he said, "Yeah, I know." (He knows! Eep!) Then — here's the best part — he smiled! It was a nice smile. It was! This led me to one conclusion:

Brown Hair + Green Eyes + Nice Smile
= The Cootie Catcher Is Right!

I know he's not my boyfriend yet, but . . .

My prediction: He will be!

Friday, September 7
Mrs. Hill's room / 7:45 a.m.

"How's it going with your new boyfriend?" asked Maybelline. She happened to be emerging from her mom's

Mercedes SUV at the same time I was prying myself from the back of my neighbor's ten-year-old Honda. So we ended up walking toward the school at the exact same time. Talk about bad luck!

Maybelline is like the White Witch from The Chronicles of Narnia: extremely beautiful, but a total ice queen. Her question gave me cold chills of dread. Last year, she asked my boyfriend, Evan, to the spring dance while we WERE STILL DATING. When he broke up with me about thirty seconds after that, it was like the worst day of my life! So if I *did* have a boyfriend, which I don't (yet), the last person I'd want to know about it would be Maybelline.

My mind raced ahead as we walked forward, trying to think of all of the possible ways she could have heard about my crush on Malcolm. The only person who knew was Kara, and she would NEVER tell Maybelline something like that. Never! And Maybelline isn't even in band, so there's no way she could deduce I like him by watching me or something. Therefore, she couldn't possibly know about my crush!

I responded with confidence. "I don't have a boyfriend, Colleen."

"Oh? That's not what I heard." She paused to whip a tube of lip gloss from her bag.

I was tempted to keep walking, but of course I *just had to know* what she'd heard. I don't know why I felt this way. It's not like she's ever said a single thing to me that made me feel good.

"Really. I don't," I said, hoping it was enough for her to spill.

"I heard you were in love with Pizza Face."

This confused me. Pizza Face is not a very nice name. It means someone with bad acne, but I couldn't think of a single guy in my class who fit that description. "Who'd you hear that from?" I asked.

"Actually" — she slid the tube of gloss across her already perfect lips — "from you. At Triple Slice last Friday. You were kinda drooling all over him."

The cold chills of dread were turning into icicles of dread and they were stabbing me in the gut. Because even though seeing a guy's head in the triple-cheese topping is a *completely normal* thing to get excited about, it occurred to me for the first time that I might have seemed a teeny bit crazy to onlookers.

Why does Maybelline always have to be at the wrong place at the right time?

I stood up extra-straight, looked ahead, and lifted my chin. Maybe it was a mistake to drool over pizza cheese guy in a public place . . . but I couldn't admit that to Maybelline. At this point I only had one choice: to own it.

I glanced back at her and picked up my pace. "Oh, I'm *over* him!" I called, laughing like it was a big joke and hoping it looked like I didn't care *what* she saw. Or said. Maybe that way she'll never bring it up again.

Cafeteria / 12:16 p.m.

Mr. Gheary is a totally cool nerd! Today we played *another game* to teach us about probability. It is called Pig Out and it's played with dice. Dianna Leroy was my partner this time, and I beat her two out of three games. At the end of class, Mr. G announced (after a dramatic pause, of course) that we'd be getting a big assignment on using probability to predict the future. He said he'll give us details Monday.

Since I'm already pretty good at predicting the future with things like the pizza cheese guy and the cootie catcher, I can make a prediction about this assignment.

My prediction: I'm gonna rock it! (Not to be confused with "I'm gonna rocket!")

Uncool Carpool / 3:00 p.m.

Today, in band, the best thing ever happened. Malcolm, the boy who never talks, came up to *me* and asked *me* if I was going to the skate park on Sunday.

No, I hadn't *planned* to go to the skate park.

Yes, plans change!

So I told him I'd meet him there. I'm not sure if this counts as our first date, but I'm counting it anyway!

I pretty much couldn't concentrate on anything after that. My mind was too busy imagining myself whizzing down ramps, hand in hand with my future boyfriend.

Family room / 5:08 p.m.

Kara says I can't count going to the skate park as a date unless something happens.

"What kind of SOMETHING?" I asked.

"Gah!" she said, smiling. "Do I have to spell everything out for you?" She grabbed a piece of paper and made me a diagram.

What Counts as a Date

his arm around
your shoulders

hand holding

sharing a shake

any kissing...
even a cheek kiss

asking for a future date

defending his territory

I suggested Kara and Chip come along for moral support, but she already had plans to go visit her grandmom. She did give me one piece of advice, though.

"Whatever you do, Tabs," she said, "promise me you won't try to skate."

"Why?" I asked, a little hurt.

"Face it, Tabs," said Kara. "You're a wimp."

"A wimp!" I gaped at her. "I am SO not a wimp!"

"I mean, you're not a wimp about most things . . ." said Kara, ". . . just *some* things. Things involving any type of pain, for example. Since you've never been on a skateboard before, you'll fall if you try. And that will be painful. Then you'll cry."

"Thanks for your faith in me," I said.

Kara put her hands on my shoulders and looked into my eyes. "I have tons of faith in you. Once you put your mind to something, you never back down. I know this, too. So please don't put your mind to trying to skateboard in front of a guy you have a crush on."

"If I get hurt trying to skateboard . . . Oh. Well. I can take it." I backed up so that her hands slipped from my shoulders and dangled at her sides.

"Right," said Kara, crossing her arms. "Like you could take it last week when I stepped on your toe."

"You were wearing shoes and I wasn't! It really hurt!" I said.

"I was wearing *bedroom slippers*!" Kara reminded me. "And you almost cried last month when you got that tiny little cut on your chin."

"Who could have predicted I had a dangerous weapon in my hands? It was deceptively sharp."

"Sharp? It was a day-old roll from Panera Bread!"

"It *bled*! Doesn't everyone almost cry when they're bleeding?"

"No," said Kara. She shook her head.

In the end, I did promise not to try skateboarding. *This* time.

"Good," said Kara. "Because it's better to look good from the sidelines than to get out there and kill your chances with your crush."

Humph! I hate it when Kara is right! I am still excited about going, though. Now I only have to convince Mom to let me. That could be harder than learning to pop an ollie.

My room / 9:12 p.m.

After negotiations worthy of Congress, Mom said she'd drop me off at the skate park for an hour on Sunday if I agreed to her conditions. (Like I had any choice!) To make sure we were clear about her conditions, she wrote them down on the magnetic notepad stuck to the fridge.

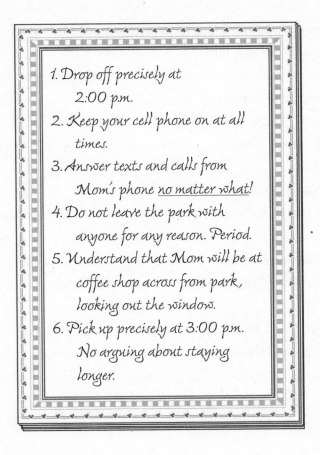

1. Drop off precisely at 2:00 p.m.
2. Keep your cell phone on at all times.
3. Answer texts and calls from Mom's phone _no matter what!_
4. Do not leave the park with anyone for any reason. Period.
5. Understand that Mom will be at coffee shop across from park, looking out the window.
6. Pick up precisely at 3:00 p.m. No arguing about staying longer.

Oh. Well. It's better than nothing.

My prediction: The skate park is still gonna rock!

Saturday, September 8
My room, more specifically, my bed / 8:27 a.m.

Oh no. Oh no no no no no! I feel terrible. I mean really awful. My stomach is flipping faster than a gymnast on a trampoline. My skin feels like it did that time I spent a day at Lake Whitmore and forgot sunscreen. My throat feels like that, too. It's on fire.

My plan is to lie here quietly in bed without moving. At all. If I move, I might throw up. Fever, I can hide from Mom. Vomit, not so easily, since it usually comes with unpleasant sound effects and a nasty aroma.

If she finds out I'm sick there's NO WAY she'll let me go to the skate park tomorrow! But if I just lie here, maybe she'll think I'm just having a lazy Saturday. Then by tomorrow I might be better anyway. Hope. Hope. Hope.

Haven't moved / 1:34 p.m.

The problem with being an only child is that your mom has WAY too much time to pay attention to your every move. When she checked in with me this morning, I told her I was sleeping in. She seemed fine with that. But I guess after 10:30 a.m. it isn't okay to be lazy anymore. Because that's when Mom came in, put her hand on my head, and declared me "sick as a dog."

"What, suddenly you're a doctor? Or a vet?" I asked.

"Honey, you're burning up."

"But I can still go to the skate park tomorrow, right?"

Mom looked doubtful. "Maybe. *If* you don't have a fever in the morning . . ."

"I won't!" I promised. I sure hope I can keep that promise!

Sunday, September 9
My stinkin' room / 11:21 a.m.

After I threw up the ginger ale and toast Mom brought me, I decided I felt a lot better. I went downstairs to tell her the good news. She took one look at me and pointed back up the stairs. Completely unfair!

I might as well have fallen off of a skateboard, because this really did make me cry! I'm going to stand Malcolm up before I even get a chance to date him! I guess I just have to hope that he's a very understanding guy. . . .

Mom came in to bring me soup and saw that I'd been crying. When I told her why, she offered to drive over to the skate park, find Malcolm, and explain why I wasn't there. I asked my internal Mortification Meter how I'd feel about that. It took about half a second to get the results.

I'm definitely gonna have to take my chances on the *understanding guy* thing.

Monday, September 10
Same old room / 7:10 a.m.

I feel fine! Why doesn't anyone believe me? There's no point in missing school (and a chance to explain to Malcolm where I was yesterday). But Mom whipped out the thermometer and let *it* decide!

No fair! A machine can't tell how you really feel. My temp was only 101! That's barely any fever at all. When I heard Mom call her firm to explain why she wouldn't be there today, I knew arguing was useless. She never misses work.

Three guesses / 3:15 p.m.

Kara called and said I didn't miss much today. She made me feel better about Malcolm, too, by saying she was sure he'd understand.

The great news is that I haven't had a fever since before lunch!

My prediction: Tomorrow I'll get a rain check on my "date."

Tuesday, September 11
My room / 7:10 a.m.

Woke up feeling much better! Got dressed in a hurry and ran down to tell Mom, who said I must have had a twenty-four-hour bug. Twenty-four-hour? I missed out on *three days of my life*! Even *I* know that's seventy-two hours.

*Note to future self: Don't get Mom's accounting firm to do my future taxes.

Mom felt my forehead and held my face in her hands for a moment. "Okay, Tabbi, you can go back. If you start feeling bad, call me."

I started feeling bad about thirty seconds later. I was in the middle of brushing my teeth when I saw it. I mean *zit* — a huge one — spreading across my cheek like alien slime trying to take over the surface of a new planet. I guess that's what I get from those two days of not getting ready in front of a mirror. Plenty of time for a zit invasion to catch me off guard.

It was ginormous. I turned my head to the side. Holy guacamole! I swear the thing changed my profile. I grabbed a washcloth, soaked it in hot water, and scrubbed. Pointless!

"Tab-i-thaaaaaa! Hurry up! Your ride gets here in five minutes." Mom sounded urgent, as always. I looked back into the mirror. I only had one choice.

"Mom! I'm feeling awful! I'd better stay at home another day."

Mom came charging up the stairs. "What's wrong?" She sounded panicked. Then her eyes took in my clown-nose-red cheek.

"Is this about that little pimple?"

"It's not little! There are radishes smaller than this thing! I can't go to school like this!"

"Sure you can," said Mom. "It's normal to have pimples at your age." She grabbed a tube of concealer and began attacking the invader.

She definitely didn't understand, so I tried desperately to explain. "If anyone sees me today, they'll have an image of *this*" — I pointed to my cheek — "in their head for the REST OF THEIR LIFE."

I remembered the image that comes to my head every time I see Frankie Ziegler.

When we were in kindergarten, Frankie was FAMOUS. He had this weird talent for putting rocks in his nose. His nostrils stretched out bigger and bigger and bigger with each rock he added.

Frankie was the hit of the playground. While the teachers weren't looking, we'd watch him try to beat his record of five rocks per nostril with the kind of fascination everyone has for a totally normal-looking person who does freaky things.

But one day Frankie experienced expanding-nostril FAIL! The rocks that he'd stuffed *into* his nose would not come back *out*.

Frankie thought the teacher wouldn't notice him if he carried his lunch box in front of his face.

But it was kind of hard for Mrs. Malloy not to notice Frankie's giant nose! His unhappy dad came to get him about an hour later.

The next day Frankie came to school wearing a hospital bracelet. He'd gone to the ER to get those stuck rocks removed!

I know it's hard to believe, but this experience didn't affect Frankie's nose permanently. He has a completely normal-sized nose today.

Frankie Now

Still, every time *I* look at Frankie, I see him with that humongous nose. It's like my brain puts a *Frankie on his stupidest day ever* mask on top of what he looks like now.

Nostril-fail Frankie

Frankie goes to the other county middle school now, and last time I saw him, I thought he looked pretty cute. Then that big-nosed mask floated from my brain to cover his face and I had an EWWWW moment.

I couldn't let something like that happen to me!

I looked right at Mom. "If you make me go to school today, it could *ruin my life*!"

Uncool Carpool / 7:30 a.m.

I guess Mom isn't too worried about ruining my life.

I'm in the backseat of Mrs. Winston's car, with a giant flesh-colored lump on my cheek. I can now see why Mom chose public accounting instead of a career that involves stage makeup.

Usually I can't wait to get out of this old Honda where I have to squeeze between toddler Jimmy and his sticky applesauce fingers and Addie the sixth grader. Today, however, I dread the moment this car rolls to a stop.

For the first time since I got it all cut off, I wish I had my long blond hair back. Then I could just chew on the ends all day, looking absentminded, while discreetly covering the zit with my hair. Geez. Short hair leaves you so vulnerable sometimes!

At least I had the last-minute idea to throw on my Rasta hat with the fake dreads attached. I can always chew on one of those to cover my cheek!

What? I've worn it to school before. In third grade. On hat day. But still.

Mrs. Hill's room / 7:40 a.m.

Kara made me ditch the Rasta hat. She said it only drew attention to me because of its bright colors. She also made the point that:

Chewing on Your Own Hair = Nervous Looking

But:

Chewing on Fake Dread = Crazy Looking

I am soooooooo thankful that it's an "A" day today. No band! I'm desperate to explain to Malcolm where I was on Sunday, but not desperate enough to talk to him until this zit disappears, or at least shrinks, like, majorly.

Library / 12:05 p.m.

Me and my giant zit plan to spend the entire lunch period here at one of the back tables, where I'm least likely to see Malcolm. Or anyone else.

Anyway, now's a good time to write about the algebra DISASTER. See, when Kara said I hadn't missed much yesterday, I didn't worry. But I'd forgotten one thing. She's not in my algebra class, so she didn't realize I'd missed something HUGE.

YESTERDAY they picked partners for Mr. G's crazy probability project that he told us about on Friday! UGH! So of course everyone cool was already paired up with other cool people. Which left the uncoolest person of all for me. She came rushing toward me, blinding me with her hot pink *Cute as a Cupcake, Sweet as Icing* T-shirt and glittery Toms.

"Tabbi, I am so excited to work with you as my partner! Doesn't this project sound like so much fun? We can predict so many great things! I have tons of ideas, don't you, Tabbi? I can't wait to try them out, can you?"

"Uh . . . I haven't really had time to think about it much since I was sick and all, Priyanka," I said, smiling even though my brain was frowning. In fact, my brain was kinda talking to me at that point, so I didn't hear the next few sentences Priyanka said.

"No worries," said Priyanka cheerfully. "I have tons of ideas! I'll start with the best one: We can use cupcakes for our probability project!" She pumped her fist in the air. It slammed into James's arm as he walked by. He stepped back and scowled at her. For the first time ever, Priyanka looked wilted.

I know she's annoying, but it was clearly an accident. I didn't think it was fair of James to make her feel bad. What a jerk! He should know by now that:

$$\frac{(\text{Priyanka} \times \text{Any Kind of Excitement}) + (\text{Person Passing within Three Feet of Her})}{\text{SMACK!}}$$

If James can't learn that simple formula, I don't know how he expects to pass algebra this year!

"So how, exactly, can we use cupcakes for our probability project?" I asked, trying to help Pri focus on something besides James's glower.

Priyanka rubbed her hands together like she was super-excited. She bounced up and down on her heels. The cupcake-shaped earrings in her ears swung back and forth. "Get this," she said. "We can predict what kind of cupcake people will like most."

"Chocolate," I said. "Since we've figured that out, I guess we're done with our project."

"Tabbi, you are so funny!" she said. She laughed so loudly that it sounded fake. But it definitely wasn't. Jake Baxter turned around in his desk and stared at us. Since I didn't want anyone staring at me on the day of the giant zit invasion, I needed to say something to get Pri to stop laughing.

"Why don't we get together after school sometime and try to come up with a project we'll both like," I suggested.

"Great idea!" she said. "I'll come over right after school today!"

"Tomorrow," I put in quickly. "I have this . . . thing . . . today."

"Okay, tomorrow! And we can bake cupcakes to help us brainstorm!"

"Uhhh . . . sure," I said, because I was kinda taken off guard and couldn't think of what else to say.

So now I have until tomorrow to A) convince Mom to buy

baking supplies and let me mess up the kitchen and B) come up with something better than cupcakes to do our probability project on.

My prediction: Our project is going to stink!

Uncool Carpool / 3:01 p.m.

Got through the whole day without seeing Malcolm. I'm DYING to explain why I wasn't there Sunday, but

$$Zit^{27} + Malcolm\ Encounter = \heartsuit\ Disaster!$$

Why didn't we exchange phone numbers? Then I could let him know why I didn't show up from the safe distance of my cell!

My room / 4:00 p.m.

As soon as I got home I attacked my cheek with Clearasil. Then I called Kara to tell her about the algebra disaster.

Me: I got the worst partner for my algebra project.

Kara: Who? Not Maybelline; she took it last year with me.

Me: Worse.

Kara: No one's worse than Maybelline.

Me: At least she's cool.

Kara: You mean at least she *thinks* she's cool. So who do you have for your partner? Not James? That'd be awkward.

Me: I'd prefer awkward to what I got.

Kara: Who is it already? Spill.

Me: Priyanka Gupta.

There was a long pause, like Kara was trying to think of what to say.

Kara: What's wrong with her? She seems nice.

Me: Hmmmm. I guess. But she wants to use our probability project to predict the most popular flavor of cupcake.

Kara: Chocolate.

Me: I know, right? I told her that. So what's the point predicting something everyone already knows?

Kara: Don't worry too much, Tabs — she's really nice. I'm sure you can talk her out of it.

Me: Got any ideas? She's coming over tomorrow to bake cupcakes and talk about it.

Kara (laughing): Well, you could always try to predict which flavor soil earthworms like best.

Me: Ha. Didn't that project already fail for you?

Kara: It was an F-plus! (laughs) But it was for a different teacher, anyway.

Me: Well, thanks for the suggestion, but I'll try to come up with my own idea.

Kara: If I think of anything, I'll call you.

Me: Good. Do that. I'll be waiting for your call.

My room / 9:10 p.m.

Still waiting for Kara's call.

Wednesday, September 12
Mrs. Hill's room / 7:41 a.m.

The good news is that my cheek looks almost normal today. Almost.

It still has a spot on it as red as a bull's-eye. But at least the spot is like the plains instead of the mountains. I mean, today the concealer actually concealed it . . . almost. So I put extra makeup on, including mascara to draw attention to my eyes, and lip gloss to draw attention to my lips, hoping that all the attention my eyes and lips will get means the shrinking spot on my cheek will be ignored.

I came to school with a three-point mission.

1. Seek Malcolm out.
2. Explain why I wasn't there Sunday.
3. Arrange another skate-park "date."

Unfortunately, I only accomplished one of those points. I absolutely positively couldn't wait until band to talk to Malcolm, so I walked around campus trying to find him before the first bell.

I found him, all right. Leaning against a locker with his arm around The Vine!

Kara and I call Gina Johns *The Vine* because she's always clinging to some guy. This time, she was clinging to the guy I had predicted would be Mr. Right. *My* Mr. Right. Suddenly everything seemed wrong.

Was Malcolm dating The Vine? If so, how long had they been going out? Before he asked me out? Since yesterday? I didn't know. And I didn't really want to find out.

I abandoned my three-point mission and texted Kara while hurrying off to class.

Me: Malcolm was w/The Vine!

Kara: As in?

Me: Leaning on locker, embracing

Kara: ☹

Me: Should I tell him bout Sun?

Kara: No. Blow him off

Me: ☹

Kara: Yr only choice

Me: I dread band

Kara: It will b okay

This time, I hope Kara is right.

My prediction: When baking cupcakes with Priyanka is the only thing you have to look forward to, it's going to be a rotten day.

Uncool Carpool / 3:03 p.m.

Managed to get through band without looking at, talking to, or otherwise interacting with Malcolm. That's what he gets! But still it makes me sad. ☹

Newly cleaned kitchen / 6:43 p.m.

The cupcake-baking session didn't go as badly as I expected, although at first it was a little awkward. When I opened the door for her, Priyanka was her usual bouncy self, wearing a bright yellow shirt that said *Make Cupcakes, Not War.*

"Hi, Tabs!" she said.

I cringed inwardly. I mean, Tabs is what Kara calls me, but no one else. I didn't think I could handle being called Tabs by Priyanka. I couldn't think of anything to say, so I ended up going with the brutal truth.

"Um, no one calls me Tabs but Kara. It's kind of a best-friend nickname," I explained as nicely as I could.

Priyanka's smile dimmed the tiniest bit, but it was still bright as day. "Okay, Tabbi," she said. "But you can call me Pri. It's what my friends call me."

I didn't have the heart to tell her we were *project partners*, not friends. The brutal truth can only rear its head so often.

"Great," I said, showing her into the kitchen.

Mom surprised me by enthusiastically agreeing to let us use her spotless kitchen to bake. She set out big bowls, wooden spoons, measuring cups and the mixer, along with flour, sugar, salt, vanilla, and butter. She'd even printed out a recipe for us to try.

I handed it to Pri. She looked at it and wrinkled her nose. "It's plain vanilla."

"I know. Supposedly, it's hard to mess up plain vanilla."

"Well," said Pri, "let's start with this recipe, then add a little of this and a little of that. It's what makes baking fun . . . you know . . . not being able to predict exactly how something will turn out."

"I thought the whole point of this project was to predict exactly how something will turn out."

Pri shrugged her narrow shoulders. "Sure, but that's a boring way to bake, and since we're baking for inspiration, let's just tweak when the inspiration hits!"

"Okay . . ." I said. "But you'll have to do most of the tweaking. I haven't baked much before."

"Poor Tabbi," said Pri, patting my shoulder. Her big brown-black eyes were full of pity.

"It's okay," I said.

Pri's huge smile reappeared. Her eyes twinkled. "Ha-ha-ha! I was kidding. But you've been missing out on all of the fun!"

So we got busy making the batter. Then Pri added an extra half teaspoon of vanilla to the bowl. No big deal, I know. But after we poured the golden batter into the cupcake liners, she did something far less predictable. She grabbed a bag of snack-sized Oreos and shoved one right down into the batter of each cupcake!

"We'll call this recipe Oreo Surprise," she said. "Wait. No. That name would ruin the effect."

I had to laugh. Pri can be really funny! And she was right about one thing: I *had* been missing out on all of the fun.

Here's what one of the cupcakes we made looked like when we finished:

It tasted as good as it looked!

But here's what Mom looked like when we she saw the kitchen:

I guess we shouldn't have left those batter-covered dishes in the sink.

I'm sure when Mom cools down, sees how great I cleaned the kitchen, and tastes the Oreo Surprise cupcakes, she'll get over the mess.

My room / 8:00 p.m.

Mom is not over the mess. When I asked if Pri could come over again tomorrow she said NO without even letting me get the whole sentence out of my mouth. Obviously she hasn't tasted those delicious cupcakes yet.

She was in such a bad mood that I came up here early. Being around Mom was bringing me DOWN!

Anyway, despite Malcolm dumping me before we could even go out, Mom being in a rotten mood, and Pri and me still not having a probability project, I'm in a strangely *good* mood! Maybe it has something to do with having that yummy smell back in the house.

I flipped open my algebra notebook, hoping a project idea would leap off of the pages and into my brain. And that's kinda what happened when I read this sentence:

Probability can help you predict possible outcomes. If you gather information accurately, it's possible to help you control some of them.

When Mr. Gheary told us this, he explained how some companies use probability to improve business. They study the buying patterns of people, and then use the data to predict which products will lead to increased sales.

Well, I don't need to increase sales. I need to increase my chances of finding a boyfriend. But . . . what if instead of studying consumer buying patterns, I studied teen dating patterns? If I did that, I could use the collected data to increase my chances of finding a boyfriend! Why can't we do our probability project on something like that? Hey — it worked for Kara last year. She basically used a science project to find Chip! I could use a probability project to solve my boy problem!

I started wondering . . . what kinds of things can a girl do to increase her probability of finding a boyfriend? Would wearing more makeup help? It seems to work for Maybelline. Does getting in touch with him through texting or Faceplace help? Do your chances of finding a boyfriend increase if you act a certain way?

I don't even have time to write down all of the questions crowding into my head. It's too late. The sky is like black velvet now, providing a perfect background for the hopeful light of the stars to twinkle against. If I leave my bedroom curtains open, maybe one of them will shoot across the blackness, and I can make a wish on it before I fall asleep.

Thursday, September 13
Mrs. Hill's room / 7:42 a.m.

In an effort to cheer me up, Kara showed up at school with her own (lame) version of the love-predictor cootie catcher.

It had these serious statements on it, like "Your crush looks deeply into your eyes when he talks to you," and "Your crush doesn't mind when you spend time with your friends," and "Your crush is kind to his mother."

Seriously? I'm having a hard time just meeting guys, never mind meeting their moms to see how they're treated!

"The problem with yours, Tabs, was that your choices

were superficial," Kara explained. "You can't base a relation-ship on someone's eye color."

"I wasn't basing a relationship on that; I was *using* eye and hair color to make a *prediction!*"

She gave me that look. The one that said *same thing.* Then she held out her cootie catcher toward me. "Go ahead," she said. "TRY it."

I tried it. Kara wrote down my results and handed them to me:

Kara's cootie catcher's prediction: The guy for you listens when you talk, answers texts, and remembers special days like your birthday.

I looked at the piece of paper in my hand. "How am I sup-posed to find this guy, huh? Nothing here gives me a clue as to what he might look like."

"That's the whole point!" said Kara. "You have to *get to know* someone before you can tell if this prediction is true or not. But if you find a guy like that, he's a keeper."

"This guy sounds a lot like Chip."

Kara swatted my arm with her duct-tape handbag. "Don't even think about it!"

Because we're BFFs, I didn't tell her not to worry. There's not a chance that I'd ever think about Chip as a potential boyfriend. He's nice but too goofy! LOL!

Cafeteria / 12:01 p.m.

We had a sub last period, so I sat in Maybelline's usual seat behind Kara. (Maybelline moved next to Alex B, of course.)

I showed Kara the notes I made last night for a boyfriend probability project.

"I like the way you're thinking!" she said. "You might discover that something totally within your control, like sending a text, can seriously increase your chances."

I nodded, hoping it really would work that way. "Should I try to get more information by doing some sort of survey like you did last year?"

"Sure. Why not?" said Kara. So we started making up a survey to post to Faceplace, instead of reading about photosynthesis.

For middle school girls ONLY! Help with this survey by answering these questions:

Questions

1. **Have you ever had a boyfriend?**
   - ○ Yes
   - ○ No

If yes, keep reading. If no, you are done. Thanks and bye!

2. **Did you do anything at all to get your BF to notice you?**
   - ○ Yes
   - ○ No

If yes, keep reading. If no, you are done. Thanks and bye!

3. **I started wearing more makeup to get the attention of the guy I wanted to date.**
   - ○ True
   - ○ False

4. **I got my boyfriend to notice me by contacting him through:**
   - ○ Texting
   - ○ Faceplace
   - ○ Message from a friend
   - ○ I did not contact him before he became my boyfriend.

5. Did you use a form of physical contact to get the guy you liked to notice you?

○ Yes

○ No

If yes, keep reading. If no, you are done. Thanks and bye!

6. The form of physical contact I used to get him to notice me was:

○ "Accidentally" bumping into him

○ Touching his arm when talking to him

○ Hugging him whenever I saw him

○ Other

I can't wait to see how girls answer! Kara said she'd show me how to upload the survey to Faceplace this weekend. This will make an awesome probability project! I was so excited, I sent Pri a text:

Me: Have great idea 4 prob proj

Pri: ??????

Me: Boys!

Pri: ???

Me: I'll explain later

Pri: Let's bake together again, then decide

Me: Okay

Hmmm. Maybe Pri is trying to stall me — like I was try-ing to stall her. I'm sure when I explain how awesome this can be, she'll get excited about it, though, like she does about everything!

Band room (actually, a practice room) / 2:30 p.m.

Just when I had a plan to forget Malcolm and move on with my probability prediction, he called me over to him during band. He was tapping his drumstick casually on the snares. My heart was tapping, not so casually, in my chest. "Where were you Sunday?" he asked.

I couldn't believe it. Maybe I should've explained where I was, but his question caught me off guard. Instead, I blurted out, "When I saw you in the hall with Gina, it didn't *look* like you missed me on Sunday."

He smiled. His smile was really nice. Nice and mysterious. His green eyes peeped at me from beneath his hang-bang. I felt a rush of excitement. Maybe The Vine was his cousin or something! Maybe he was being a supportive family member. Maybe there was still a chance that he was *the one!* Maybe my boy problem was about to be solved.

But then he said, "Well, she was there Sunday and you weren't." What, exactly, did *that* mean? If I *had* been there, would his arm have been draped over *my* shoulders instead of The Vine's? Is *that* all that relationships boil down to — being in the right place at the right time? I was too stunned to reply.

I started backing away toward my seat, but my heel caught the feet of the cymbal stand. I had a **slow-mo**tion **mo**ment.

The cymbal made this obnoxious clattering noise as it fell over next to me on the floor. Like the universe clanging out a warning: *He's not the one! He's not the one!*

To his credit, I guess, Malcolm offered a hand to help me up. But I was so mad, and so embarrassed, that I just glared at him and helped myself up.

My head was reeling. And the silence in the room seemed to amplify this. It was a very loud silence, if you know what I mean — except for the ringing of the cymbal bouncing from the walls, signaling everyone to *LOOOOOOOOOK AT TAB-IIIIIIIII-THAAAAAAA!!!!*

As for me, I didn't look at anyone. I couldn't bear for my eyes to see any smirking smiles or even sympathy. Plus, I was kinda afraid I'd start crying, because falling flat on your butt on the band room floor REALLY HURTS!

So I held my head up high and strolled back to the flute section like nothing happened. But why does the flute section have to be *all the way* at the front of the class?

When my face cooled off and my heart stopped racing, I asked for a restroom pass, which I used to escape into this closet-like practice room. I think I'll wait until after the dismissal bell to leave . . . less chance of having to face Malcolm again!

My prediction: The Vine and Malcolm will only last as long as she doesn't let him go to the skate park without her.

Uncool Carpool / 2:57 p.m.

It seems like the sky is the world's largest mood ring and it's currently displaying my mood to the entire world. Dark gray clouds are traveling across its light gray surface, and not a speck of sun is showing encouraging light. Mr. G said this was because the storm of the millennium was about to hit the United States.

But he quickly clarified that it looked like the wind and rain were booking it to New England, so it probably wouldn't affect us much since we're basically a twelve-hour drive from there. In other words, I can't count on school being canceled tomorrow, so I need to go ahead and do my algebra homework! Phooey.

My day went from *crush-dissing, cymbal-crashing, falling-on-butt* bad to truly horrible. So horrible that I don't even care anymore about the *crush-dissing, cymbal-crashing, falling-on-butt* day I had. So horrible that it made me realize I've spent WAY too much time worrying about things that really don't matter.

I realized this almost as soon as Mom came tearing into the house like *she* was the storm of the millennium. She flung her keys and laptop bag to the floor, then raced around looking frantic. When she started hurling sofa cushions across the room, I knew something was seriously wrong.

"What are you *doing*?" I asked.

"Looking for the dang remote! Why can't you *ever* put it back where it belongs?" (When she said *ever*, she threw a pillow all the way into the dining room. I don't think that's why they're called throw pillows.)

I started looking around. I tried to remember who'd watched TV last so I could decide whether to blame Mom or slink out of the room. Then I noticed Mom's tear-filled eyes. That scared me. I'd seen her cry a couple of times — when she and Dad were splitting up, and when our cat got hit by a pickup truck — but I'd never seen her cry over something dumb like a remote.

I walked over and put my arm around her. "Why is the remote so important?"

"Because of Uncle Mike."

"He's on TV?" That was kind of exciting! I could see why Mom wanted to see her brother on TV, but not why she was so upset about it.

Mom shook her head. "I hope he's not on TV. I hope he's safe at home. I mean not home. I hope he's not at home, but that he's safe."

She wasn't making sense. I led her toward the recliner. Then I turned on the TV the hard way — with my finger! The screen flickered awake. "What channel?"

"The Weather Channel," said Mom.

I pushed the CHANNEL button about forty times until I got down to channel eighteen. A man in a raincoat appeared. He was taking a real rain-and-wind beating. Mom scooted to the edge of her seat.

"Mom, what's going on?" I asked.

"Shhhhhh."

Raincoat guy was reporting from a small town in New England. The one right next to the town where Mom grew up. I recognized the name because we pass through there every single summer on our way to visit Uncle Mike. He's my mom's only family.

A crashing wave of realization hit me! That hurricane was pounding down right on top of my uncle, aunt, and cousin! No wonder Mom was upset!

Mr. Gheary sure was wrong when he said the storm wouldn't affect us much. It's affecting us already.

Scenes flashed across the screen, showing underwater streets and power lines sparking big blue explosions. Mom pulled a tissue from her pocket and twisted it in her hands. Little white flakes fell to the carpet like dandruff.

"Is Uncle Mike okay?" I asked.

Mom's eyes were red. "They went to a shelter."

"But are they safe there?"

"Should be."

That didn't sound great to me. "What do you mean? Are they safe or not?" I was particularly worried about my cousin Maddie. She's in third grade and really tiny.

"Mike called me to say they'd arrived at a shelter and not to worry."

"So why are you worried?"

"Because what if they didn't go to a shelter far enough away from the storm? What if something happens to them while they're there? What if the roof blows off of the shelter?"

"Mom, why don't you just send Uncle Mike a text and see if he's okay?"

"I *have* sent him a text. I've sent ten! He's not answering!" Mom was practically screaming in frustration. I knew she wasn't directing it at me, but it still didn't feel very good to be yelled at.

"Maybe he's annoyed with you for texting so much," I said.

"I AM NOT ANNOYING!" Mom threw down the rest of her tissue and stomped to the kitchen. I was tempted to follow her and list the ways she's very annoying, but obviously this wasn't the right time. (Yeah, like there'll ever be a right time for that!)

"Maybe a cell tower is down and he isn't getting your texts!" I yelled after her.

This must have made her feel better, because she came back to her seat. "You're probably right, Tabitha. Thanks. I'm sure he'll be okay." Her eyes were glued to the set again. I got up and hugged her quickly, then went to the kitchen to make mac and cheese. Mom didn't look like she was in good enough shape to cook. Hopefully, by the time dinner is ready, she'll have heard from Uncle Mike.

My room / 11:30 p.m. (Normally, I'd totally celebrate a "late" bedtime like this, but not tonight.)

I spent most of the evening on the sofa with Mom, watching the Weather Channel while a knot in my stomach grew into a giant hard lump. Things in New England looked *bad*.

My cousin Maddie is afraid of thunderstorms. She must be scared to death huddled in a shelter while screaming wind and pounding rain rage over her. We still haven't heard from Uncle Mike.

I've been trying to sleep, but it's hard. I keep looking around my bedroom at my giant stuffed cat, my earring tree, and my framed pictures of family. The only ones in the house of me, Mom, and Dad together. What if I had to leave everything I loved and go to a shelter, not knowing if I'd ever see any of it again?

My *crush-dissing, cymbal-crashing, falling-on-butt* bad day seemed a long time ago now. I don't care about Malcolm anymore. All I care about is hearing good news from my family.

Friday, September 14
My room / 6:30 a.m. Yawn.

I rushed downstairs at the first peep of the cardinals outside my window. Mom was wrapped in a blanket on the sofa, chugging coffee. I knew what that meant.

Mom + Sofa + Blanket + Coffee = Sleepless Night

I walked over and kissed her cheek. She had a bad case of bedhead and was still wearing the clothes she wore to work yesterday. And I somehow feel disloyal to my mom revealing this, but I think it'd been over twenty-four hours since a toothbrush had seen the inside of her mouth. This gave me a clue to what her day would be like today.

Bedhead + Morning Breath + Wrinkled Clothes = No Work for Mom!

"Heard from Uncle Mike?" I asked. I knew the answer before she started shaking her head. "Try not to panic, Mom." But even as I said this, panic was rising up in me like the floodwater I was seeing on the flat screen in front of us. Flowing water created rivers out of streets, making New England townships look like Venice, Italy. Except cars were floating down the streets instead of boats, and piles of rubble were sitting where houses used to stand.

"I know it looks bad," I said, "but consider how many millions of people live up there. Chances are Uncle Mike's family is fine." I wasn't just trying to convince Mom of this. I needed to believe it, too.

Mom groaned.

"I'm staying home today," I said. "You don't need to be alone at a time like this!"

Somehow, that rallied Mom. She dragged herself from the sofa and plodded toward the kitchen, coffee cup shaking in her hand.

"Going for a refill?" I asked hopefully.

"Going to get you breakfast — you have school today!"

Poop.

Cafeteria / 12:27 p.m.

The bright blue sunny sky with its happy white clouds doesn't reflect my mood today at all. It's weird that in one part of the world, people are looking at boards sticking up like tombstones where their homes used to be, while in a cafeteria miles and miles away, other people are doing something moronic like throwing Cheetos at each other.

I peeked at the phone hidden in my lunch box. Mom promised she'd text me if she heard from Uncle Mike.

No new texts.

Band room / 1:50 p.m.

$$\frac{(\text{Uncle Mike} + \text{Aunt Sally} + \text{Maddie}) - (\text{Any information about how they are doing})}{(\text{Impossible for Tabbi to concentrate in school}) \times 1000}$$

Uncool Carpool / 2:56 p.m.

Pri reminded me before school that we still needed to bake together again to decide on a probability project. I don't know about baking . . . but she's right about one thing. We do need to decide on a probability project for algebra! Note cards stating predictions are due next Friday. A lot of cards are up on the bulletin board already. We're way behind!

I'm hoping Pri will like my idea: using the project as a way to find out if there are things a girl can do to increase her probability of finding a boyfriend. If Pri okays it, I know exactly what to write on our note card.

Using data collected from various sources, we'll predict ways a girl can increase her chances of finding a boyfriend.

Sounds pretty good, right? Oh! BRB! Just got a text!

Shoot! I hoped it'd be news from Mom, but it was only Pri. I have a feeling I'm gonna regret giving her my number.

Pri: Hi, Tabbi. How's it going?

Me (groaning inwardly): Fine

Pri: You didn't look fine in algebra. R U OK?

Me: Worried bout uncle. The hurricane hit his town.

Pri: Is he OK?

Me: Don't know

Pri: Hope u get good news

Me: Thnx. Bye

It's pretty nice of Pri to care, but still . . .

Nice < Good News from Fam

Family room / 4:12 p.m.

Mom is on the phone with Uncle Mike! Which means he's alive! I'm sitting here trying to figure out what they're talking about by writing down their conversation. Well, one side of it, anyway.

Mom: "Thank goodness you're all okay." (pause) "When will they let you go back and see the house?" (pause) "Oh no." (pause) "Terrible." (pause) "Oh, Mike, I can't imagine." (pause) "I understand, but call after you go home. Mmmm. Hug Maddie for us. Okay. Love you. Bye."

Mom sank into the recliner. She looks relieved, but very sad. I'm going to get the details.

My room / 8:46 p.m.

Mom stopped tucking me in a long time ago, but tonight she came and sat on my bed. She gave me a hug and kissed the top of my head. Even though we found out Uncle Mike's family is safe, I think the hurricane is making her feel extra-emotional. She smoothed my hair and sighed. "I can't believe your cousin's school was destroyed. I went to that school, you know."

"I know, Mom. But the important thing is that our family is safe."

Mom squeezed my arm. "So true. I wish we could do something to help. When I think about all the damage done to that little town . . ." Mom's voice got caught in her throat, so the rest of her sentence didn't make it out of her mouth.

The best thing to do seemed to be to hug her.

"I love you sooooo much," she whispered.

I guess hugging her was the right thing.

Saturday, September 15
My room / 7:55 a.m.
(AKA: CRA-Z early for a Saturday!)

I woke up to the sound of my mom's yelling voice. This is NOT my favorite way to say hello to a new day. I'd seriously rather have a rooster crowing at the foot of my bed than Mom calling me from three rooms away.

Yes, I would.

Because at the end of the crowing, the rooster would at least hop off my bed and then go on about his business. But when Mom stops calling, she keeps hanging around and gets up *in* my business. And she always wants me to *do* something. Something besides sleep, which is my preferred activity of the moment.

Peaceful Sleeping ÷ (Mom's Voice)^{100} = Grumpy Tabbi!

When she called a second time, I suddenly remembered the hurricane. I leapt out of bed. What if she had bad news about Uncle Mike? Panic closed in on me as I scrambled into the hallway.

"Tabitha, you up?" she asked, looking up at the landing. Her voice was cheerful, not upset.

"Mmmmmmhunh!" I said. My voice hadn't warmed up to being awake yet, so it sounded croaky like rusty hinges.

"Phone's for you!" Mom called again. She was waving the

house phone. I shielded my eyes from the sunlight invading our hallway and trudged downstairs.

I glanced at the clock on the wall. Seven forty-five!!!! WHO CALLS at seven forty-five on a Saturday morning? I'm one hundred percent sure that all of my friends are still sanely SLEEPING. Plus, none of them use my home number anyway. They call my cell.

I was about halfway down the stairs when it hit me. Malcolm! He'd probably realized what a jerk he'd been to ask me out and then start crushing on The Vine. I hurried down the rest of the steps, trying to think of what to say. I mean, everyone makes mistakes, right? If he asks me to the skate park again, I guess I should give him another chance. . . .

"I already said it was fine," said Mom, smiling and handing me the phone.

WHAT THE HECK? Told who? What?

"Hi, Tabbi!"

UGH! It wasn't Malcolm. Or any other boy. Pri's cheery voice was brighter than the sunlight. And more annoying. Of course it makes sense that a girl whose wardrobe consists of neon-colored T-shirts and sparkly shoes is a morning person. "Your mom told me your uncle is okay! I'm so happy to hear that. Anyway, my mom said we could bake over here today!" She sounded super-excited. Translation: She sounded completely normal — for Pri.

"I . . . uh . . ." Honestly, I couldn't think of what to say. I still wasn't fully awake, so it was like my brain was doing a mud run or something. It was still moving forward, but at one-tenth its normal speed.

"Your mom already said it was okay! See you at ten!"

"Uh . . . okay, bye."

"Byeeeeeee, Tabbiiiiii!" sang Pri, like a bird twittering.

GEEZ! Why do some people have to be so CHEERFUL all of the time? And shouldn't I have a CHOICE about going to Pri's?

Apparently not, since Mom and Pri worked out the details while I was minding my own business, doing what everyone else SHOULD HAVE BEEN DOING: SLEEPING!

My room / 4:49 p.m.

I got to Pri's house at the INSANE hour of ten o'clock this morning, half dreading the day and half looking forward to the cupcakes we'd soon be eating. Pri answered the door, wearing a cheerful yellow T-shirt that said *Baking a Change, One Cupcake at a Time*. Her shirt was so bright that it took me a minute to see the person standing behind her.

Kara!!!!!

"I knew you were feeling bad about your family and

needed cheering up," said Pri, stepping aside to let me in. "So I invited your BFF, too."

Suddenly, the day was looking as bright as Pri's shirt.

Their kitchen smelled delicious — rich and spicy — before we even started baking. When I said this, Pri said I was probably smelling curry, a sweet and savory spice blend that her mom cooks with. Lucky Pri!

Even though my mom is NOTHING like me, I somehow expected Pri's mom to be like her — loud and enthusiastic, wearing bright clothing covered with silly sayings. But her mother was quiet and . . . well, elegant. She did wear bright clothing, but it was a colorful dress called a sari, and it made her look tall and thin. I liked her the minute I met her. She swept into the kitchen with folds of colorful fabric flowing behind her, holding Pri's little brother on her hip. He had big brown eyes like Pri's.

Mrs. Gupta peeked into the mixing bowl. We were making double-chocolate cupcakes. She stuck a finger into the batter and swished out a taste.

"Priyanka, darling, this is quite good. Have you considered using a pinch of cayenne?"

"I thought about it, Ma, but I decided to go with plain cocoa powder." Pri's mother nodded as if she was seriously considering her information. After that they talked back and forth, sharing ideas. Mrs. Gupta was smiling, appreciating her daughter's input. Pri seemed just as happy getting her mother's advice. They'd obviously talked a lot about baking in that warm kitchen.

Watching them made an odd thing happen to me. A little lump of unhappiness seemed to be growing right below my rib cage, rising like a yeast roll. I thought about how much my mom wouldn't care what I thought in the kitchen, or anywhere else for that matter. How our relationship is mostly her telling me what to do.

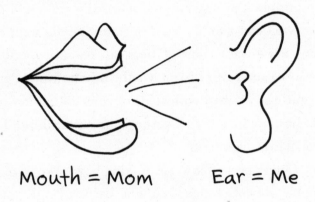

Mouth = Mom   Ear = Me

While the cupcakes were cooling, Pri's mom made us a delicious lunch — chicken with that curry spice on it and something called naan, which is flat, oval bread. I SWEAR to you it tastes as good as cupcakes! For dessert, Pri, Kara, and I each had a cupcake. They were sooo delicious that it set off an unbelievable chain of events!

First, Kara said, "Mmm. We could make a ton of money selling these."

Then my eyes landed on the words written across Pri's shirt.

Baking a Change,
One Cupcake at a Time

I felt a flash of inspiration. "Hey," I said. "We could sell cupcakes like these at our school to help raise money for my *cousin's* school. Maybe to help buy new books for their library."

Kara nodded, her eyes shining. "It'd be easy to set up a card table in the cafeteria," she suggested.

"And we could call it . . ." Pri paused to think. "Cupcakes for Catastrophes."

"Cupcakes for Catastrophes," said Kara, smiling at the idea. "That's a great name!"

"Let's use the number four instead of the word *for*, and call it C4C," I suggested.

"We should think about getting T-shirts printed with C4C on them," said Pri thoughtfully. "I'm thinking electric green."

Of course she was! But I was so thrilled with the name she'd come up with for us, I didn't even roll my eyes.

Mom had pulled into Pri's driveway, and I was heading out the door when I realized Pri and I had forgotten to do something really important.

"Our probability project!" I cried. "We spent all day together and never discussed it!"

Pri winced. "We were having so much fun that I forgot. It would make a lot of sense to do something about cupcakes now, since we'll already be baking for C4C."

"No," I said. I was not falling for that! "How about this: Since we're already kinda doing a project with cupcakes, let's use our probability project to learn about something *else*. I still want to do it on boys. Okay?"

"How can we do a project on boys?" asked Pri.

Mom tapped the horn. I've learned not to ignore that particular sound.

"I'll call you later and explain," I said. "Let's do it on boys, okay?"

Pri didn't look too excited, but she said, "Okay, call me."

When I got home and told Mom about our C4C plan, she looked about as happy as I've ever seen her look. "It's so sweet of you to think of your family like that," she said, hugging me. I'm pretty sure she was about to tear up over it, but then she got this look in her eye — the look that's always followed by one particular sentence:

"I just had another brilliant idea!"

Oof! There it was! Mom's "brilliant ideas" aren't always so brilliant, so I braced myself for the worst.

"Our firm has a program that matches funds for charities."

She grabbed her laptop and showed me the company website.

"How will this help Cupcakes 4 Catastrophes?" I asked.

"I can apply for matching funds for your project through my work, and then you'll make double the money!"

"You mean for every dollar we make, we'll actually make two? That's AWESOME." Mom's idea really *was* brilliant!

"Well . . . it's not exactly THAT simple," said Mom. Her eyebrows scrunched together and I wondered if she was thinking about the time Mr. Rinehart, a partner at her accounting firm, asked her out. My parents had only been divorced for, like, ten minutes when he'd come swooping in like a jolly old beardless Santa. He even showed up at our front door with a wrapped package (it contained oven mitts — yikes!) and a *request for the pleasure of Mom's company.*

I've never seen my got-it-together mom look so uncomfortable. She stammered something about swearing off men, then spent the next three weeks worrying about how to act at work.

"Worried Mr. Rinehart will reject our application because you rejected him?" I asked.

Mom's face got a little pink, but she waved my comment away. "No, he's not like that." She looked at the application again. "I meant it's going to take a lot of work, that's all. You'll have to make six hundred dollars on your own to get the funds," she explained.

"Not a problem," I said.

"And you'll have to do it by October 26."

Wow! That was about a month and a week away!

"Tabbi?"

"It'll be hard, but we can do it," I said.

As Mom downloaded the application, her smile was almost as big as Pri's. "I think you can, too."

MATCHING FUNDS APPLICATION

The firm of Livingston, Rinehart, and Miller is committed to making the world a better place through volunteer efforts. Employees who volunteer for charities are eligible to receive matching funds by filling out this application. To qualify, applicant is required to contribute a minimum of $600.

DEADLINE: October 26. All funds must be raised by this date.

Employee Name: Nancy Reddy

Title of Fund-raising Event: Cupcakes 4 Catastrophes

Date: September 24 through October 26

Time: lunchtime

Estimated amount you will raise: $600

Total cost of event: N/A

Estimated attendance: 400 students per day

Are you charging at the event? yes

If yes, how much? price of cupcake — approximately $1.00

Event Coordinator: Tabitha Reddy

Email: tabbigrl@wuzup.you

Provide a description of the event: A card table will be set up in the cafeteria during lunch periods Monday—Friday.

Describe how funds will be used: The funds will be used for hurricane relief, specifically to help rebuild the library at Five Corners Elementary School.

Sunday September 16
My room / 9:30 p.m.

As soon as I told Kara about the matching funds idea, she checked our school website and saw that all fund-raisers needed to be approved by our principal, Mr. O'Neal. She even went ahead and filled out the application. Kara rocks!

Then she said she had big news for me. The rest of our convo went something like this:

Me: What kind of news?

Kara: The kind you're going to love.

Me: What?

Kara: Remember Thursday, when we made that Faceplace survey?

I'd forgotten all about that! It was as if the hurricane had blown boys right out of my mind! I'd even forgotten to call Pri today to explain my boy-related probability project idea.

Me: Yeeeesssssssss?

Kara: Well, I knew you were worried about your family, so I went ahead and posted the survey for you.

Me: WHAT?

Kara: You're welcome. And if you go online now, you can check out the results.

Me: Hold on.

I flipped open my laptop, and the survey popped up in my inbox.

Total Responses to Faceplace survey: 189   **Responses**

1. Have you ever had a boyfriend?

  ○ Yes   150

  ○ No   39

If yes, keep reading. If no, you are done. Thanks and bye!

2. Did you do anything at all to get your BF to notice you?

  ○ Yes   99

  ○ No   51

If yes, keep reading. If no, you are done. Thanks and bye!

3. I started wearing more makeup to get the attention of the guy I wanted to date.

  ○ True   35

  ○ False   115

4. I got my boyfriend to notice me by contacting him through:

  ○ Texting   55

  ○ Faceplace   35

  ○ Message from a friend   18

  ○ I did not contact him before he became my boyfriend.   42

5. Did you use a form of physical contact to get the guy you liked to notice you?

  ○ Yes   89

  ○ No   61

If yes, keep reading. If no, you are done. Thanks and bye!

6. The form of physical contact I used to get him to notice me was:

  ○ "Accidentally" bumping into him   14

  ○ Touching his arm when talking to him   47

  ○ Hugging him whenever I saw him   21

  ○ Other   7

Me: Wow. A lot of these girls did things to get their boyfriends to notice them.

Kara: It's called being proactive, Tabs. Embrace it.

Me (groan): And look how many of them used physical contact to get noticed.

Kara: Works for The Vine.

Me: I can't be like her.

Kara: I know. But you have to admit that it's hard not to notice someone who's touching you, even if they just tap you on the arm.

Me: True. My problem is there are no guys at school I want to tap on the arm!

Kara: I think you'd better start looking for potential again.

Me: I guess. . . .

Kara: And this time *try* to notice at least one good thing about each guy you check out.

Me: What if there's nothing good —

Kara: Taaaaaabbiiiiiiiiiii!

Monday, September 17
In front of school / 7:31 a.m.

Kara handed me the Cupcakes 4 Catastrophes application as soon as I stepped onto campus. It looked great except for one thing. One big thing.

Spring Valley Middle Fund-raising Application

Date: _September 16_

Name of Contact Person: _Tabitha Reddy_

Email: _tabbigrl@wuzup.you_

Project Name: _Cupcakes 4 Catastrophes_

Event Hours: _Lunch every day_

Faculty Sponsor: _____

Target Audience: _Spring Valley Middle students_

Location of Event: _Cafeteria_

Donation Goal: _As much money as we can make_

How do you plan to raise funds? _We plan to bake cupcakes and sell them at lunch._

Briefly Explain how the money raised will be used:
We will send one hundred percent of the proceeds to Five Corners Elementary School. Their school was destroyed by Hurricane Franco.

"We need a faculty sponsor?!!!!!" I yelled. "Why didn't you tell me this last night?"

"'Cause I knew you'd freak out. But no worries. I'm sure we can get someone," said Kara. "Mrs. Hill might do it."

"The same Mrs. Hill who gave you detention last year?"

"Okay, so maybe not Mrs. Hill, but we'll figure it out at lunch, okay?"

We didn't have time to decide right then anyway, because the first bell rang.

Cafeteria / 12:17 p.m.

It was pretty easy to update Pri. I'd started sitting behind her in algebra so we could talk about our probability project. We only had four more days to decide on a topic and turn in our note card! Plus, sitting over on her side of the room let me get as far away from James and his stupid hands as possible!

I mean, I can't believe his GF, Kaitlin, is using the skin on his hand as her own personal canvas!!!!!

Because that's MY thing!

Now I can never write "Property of Tabbi Reddy" on another hand again, even if I do find a boyfriend, because that copycat newcomer has started writing on *her* boyfriend's hand.

I bet James put her up to it so he could flash his big fat hands around to irritate me. For the first few days of class, every single time there was an empty seat in front of me, James sat in it. Then he'd slowly raise his hand, giving me plenty of time to notice it, EVERY time he knew the answer to Mr. G's questions. And sometimes when he didn't.

And here's undeniable proof that he's using his fake hand tattoo to get my attention: The other day he PRETENDED to trip so he could "catch himself" on my desk. How convenient that his big, fat scribbled-on hand landed right under my nose so that *I couldn't help* but see his relationship status!

Well, James, your efforts to make me jealous aren't working because I am OVER YOU!

Anyway, the point is, moving to the seat behind Pri minimizes my exposure to James, even if it means I have to read T-shirts instead of hands. Today her royal-blue tee said *Just a Cupcake Looking for a Stud Muffin*. Yikes.

Before class, I filled her in on the matching-funds plan. She was so excited you'd think it was her birthday or something.

"Tabbi!" she squealed. "This is really going to happen! We will make tons of money for your cousin's library!"

"Well, I *think* it's going to happen, but we need a teacher to sponsor us, and then Principal O'Neal needs to approve it." I showed her the form with the two blank spaces.

Pri flew out of her seat like a pebble from a slingshot. I noticed, too late, that our fund-raising form had gone with her.

What I wanted to do when I saw her gesturing wildly to Mr. G, the white form flapping in her hand, was to scream.

I swear! Pri is so impulsive that she makes a squirrel look calm and calculating.

She slapped the form down on my desk triumphantly. "Now all we need is Mr. O'Neal's John Hancock!"

I didn't have to look down to know what I'd see.

"Tabbi, what's wrong?" asked Pri.

"I just wish you'd asked before getting Mr. G to be our sponsor. I mean, he's new here. I don't really even know him, do you?"

"No, but . . ."

"This is *important* to me, Pri. I don't want to mess it up by having the wrong faculty sponsor!"

"He was nice about it," said Pri in an unusually small voice.

I sighed. "How nice? What'd he say when you asked him?"

"Um, he said, 'Cupcakes? That's different from the others.'"

I groaned. "Different from the others? Why'd he say *that*?"

Pri cringed in a way that let me know I wasn't going to like the next thing out of her mouth. Not. A. Good. Sign. And when those words started coming out, they got smaller and smaller and smaller.

"I told him we were going to use cupcakes for a probability project too."

"What?" I said. I couldn't hear her. I didn't want to hear her. But I needed to hear her.

"Itoldhimweweregoingtousecupcakesforaprobability projecttoo." These words sped out of her mouth like a moon-bound rocket.

Know how you rip off a Band-Aid fast so the pain won't last long? Well, the speed of an unwelcome sentence does not reduce the pain of hearing it. Trust me.

I was steamed like a Maine lobster! Pri had just locked us in to doing the probability project *she* wanted to do when just two days ago she agreed to go along with my boy probability project idea! So now instead of using the project to find out useful, life-changing information about guys, we're stuck spending even more time with cupcakes. Things that will never love you back. Very convenient, Pri.

"On Saturday you said it'd be okay to do our probability project on boys," I reminded her.

"Yeah, but we were going to talk about it," she said, "and we never did, so . . ." Her voice trailed off.

"I guess this means you've figured out exactly how we are going to use cupcakes for our probability project?" I said.

"Well," said Pri, looking down, "I told him we were still deciding that part. I'm sure we can come up with something great."

I was glad she was sure, because I wasn't. I was about to say so, too, when Mr. G stepped up to the front of the class and started his dramatic pausing, so we had to drop the convo.

At the first tiny *ting* of the bell, I soared from my seat. I had to get AWAY from Pri. The sooner, the better. Thank goodness we didn't have any other classes together.

Despite my wishing a name besides Mr. Gheary's was on it, I went ahead and turned in the form to Mr. O'Neal before heading to lunch, where I am now, sitting across from Kara and Chip. They're ignoring me while I look engrossed in my journal. It's okay. I want to be ignored. I'm too irritated to talk. To anyone!

Grrrrrr. (That's not the grrrrrr of a territorial dog, BTW. Think bear. Kodiak bear. With cubs.)

Band room / 1:50 p.m.

Okay, I've cooled off a little. Just a little. Like a single raindrop has fallen into my steaming, angry brain.

It's hard to stay in a rotten mood when you've received one of these:

Back to
SCHOOL
BASH!!!
DIANNA'S HOUSE
FRIDAY SEPTEMBER 21
07:30 PM
BE THERE!

It's only an invitation to the BIGGEST PARTY OF THE YEAR! Dianna Leroy always has the best parties, and she said this year her parents are letting her invite almost everyone.

My room / 3:15 p.m.

Right before band, I told Kara about the Mr. Gheary sponsor thing. She didn't say anything at first.

"Pri is so clueless sometimes!" I complained.

"She really shouldn't have done that without asking," said Kara.

"I know, right?!"

Kara seemed thoughtful. "Yeah," she said, "but she was pretty great to you when you were worried about your uncle. You know, checking in on you. Inviting me to bake with you guys. Even introducing you to baking cupcakes in the first place. Without her, we wouldn't even be worried about a sponsor."

Dang. I hadn't thought about it that way.

"Still!" I said.

"You have to give her cred, Tabs," Kara went on. "I'm not thrilled about using a teacher I've never even met before as a sponsor, but we can't waste time fuming. We need to plan out how to make C4C a huge success."

When we finished talking, I realized three things:

1. I didn't want to think about C4C.
2. I wanted to stay angry.
3. Kara was right. We had to make a plan.

(Have I mentioned how much I HATE it when Kara's right?)

But I figured I didn't have to do ANYTHING until we knew whether or not Mr. O'Neal approved our fund-raiser.

What I needed right now was a distraction. And I couldn't think of anything better to distract me than boys. Pri might have made sure that we used cupcakes for our probability project, but that wasn't going to keep me from doing an *independent study*!

My prediction: My probability project on boys is gonna get some serious attention. From me!

Tuesday, September 18
Mrs. Hill's room / 7:38 a.m.

I knew an awesome place to scope out guys at my school: my locker! It's the perfect location because it's one of the first lockers on the main hallway. EVERYONE passes by it in the morning.

So before the first bell today I spent a very long time messing with things in my locker, leaning against it, and, you know, checking out the traffic. Mostly I saw guys I've already eliminated. Malcolm, for example. He still looked cute and mysterious, especially without his new accessory (The Vine). But I glanced away as soon as the green eyes beneath the hang-bang met mine.

I also saw that cute dark-haired guy I'd seen on the first day of school (the one I thought was in sixth grade). I heard him before I saw him, actually, because he was dribbling a soccer ball down the hall. It looked like he really knew what he was doing, too.

I took a good look at him as he passed by. Up close, this guy did NOT look like he was only in sixth grade. Or maybe I just didn't want him to be. His hair was gorgeous. It was fairly short, but his loopy black curls bounced when he walked. His skin was olive. He smiled and waved at someone farther down the hall, so I could see he had at least one irresistible dimple. I swear I heard birds singing. I smelled cupcakes baking. I felt the wind rushing through my short flowing hair.

He went on by me, *tap, tap, tap*ping the ball, and I watched his back for a moment, noticing how straight he held his broad shoulders. Shoulders too broad for a sixth grader? I didn't know. But I was going to find out! I felt a rush of excitement as I slammed my locker closed and started down the hall after him.

"Earth to Tabbi," said a familiar voice.

Chip was suddenly standing right in front of me. Groan. He grinned. "You were really spaced-out there. What were you thinking about?"

"You know. Stuff," I said.

"Awesome! I know tons of stuff," he joked. "For example, I know that a jellyfish is about ninety-five percent water. So why don't they call it a waterfish?"

"I don't know," I said absentmindedly. I stepped around Chip to see where Soccer Boy had gone, but it was too late.

He and the ball had both disappeared.

Cafeteria / 12:07 p.m.

Mr. O'Neal approved our fund-raiser! He said we could start Cupcakes 4 Catastrophes on Monday. Six days away. This meant we had to do a lot of planning — and baking.

I texted Pri.

Me: Mr. O says ok. Want 2 come over 2 plan?

Pri: Yes!

Me: 3:30?

Pri: Ok! I'm sorry about Mr. G

Me: k

It really wasn't okay, but we had a lot of work to do for C4C. Plus, like it or not, Pri and I still had to do a probability project together. It's hard to move forward when you're carrying around the extra weight of a grudge.

My room / 5:16 p.m.

I'm up here having a "bathroom break" because I want to write this stuff down before I forget it. Kara and Pri are still downstairs waiting for Mom. She's giving them a ride home.

We'd started planning as soon as we walked in my front door. I had good news to share. Since we were doing this to help her brother, Mom offered to donate the baking supplies. Hooray!

"Great!" said Kara. "We'll earn money faster without having to deduct costs from expenses."

"What kind of cupcakes should we bake first?" asked Pri.

"In order for our fund-raiser to make the most money possible, we need to figure out which flavors people like best," I said.

"Let's brainstorm," suggested Kara. "You know — make a list of our favorite flavors and go from there. Chocolate and vanilla for sure," she said, scribbling them down.

"And red velvet," I added.

"Hmmm," said Kara, holding the pencil still. "We probably shouldn't do red velvet *and* chocolate, since red velvet has chocolate in it."

"No way!" I couldn't believe those red-and-white cupcakes were made with chocolate.

"Way!" said Kara.

Pri was sitting on the sofa, messing around with the laptop. She hadn't contributed to our list at all up to this point. "Kara's right," she piped up. "Red velvet often calls for cocoa powder, which is chocolate."

I hate it when Kara is right!

I looked at Pri. "You said often, not always, right?"

"Usually. Cocoa powder is usually used," said Pri.

Grrrr. Still, I wasn't *exactly* wrong. Time to change the subject. "So what other flavors are popular?" I asked.

Pri shoved a piece of paper into my hand. *Most Popular Cupcake Flavors* was written across the top. Twelve different flavors were listed beneath.

"Pri," I said, rolling my eyes, "*your* favorite flavors aren't *necessarily* everyone else's favorites. We're trying to come up with a list *together*. That's what brainstorming is."

Pri put her hands on her hips. She actually looked irritated with me. Then her hands left her hips and started waving around exasperatedly. "I KNOW what brainstorming is. I Googled *favorite cupcakes* while you and Kara were arguing over stupid red velvet. This list was created after over fifteen hundred people were surveyed . . . so it should be more accurate than any list the three of us can come up with!"

I winced apologetically.

"As for the red velvet argument," Pri added, "you were *wrong* and Kara was *right*!"

Ouch.

Kara broke the ice. "Great list, Pri!" she said, pointing to it. "But pumpkin? Seriously?"

"I know, right? Who eats pumpkin cupcakes when you can have chocolate or *red velvet*?" Pri didn't look at me when she said it, but her *not looking* at me told me something: I had crossed a line with her. I needed to dive into the conversation and try to rescue our partnership. I gave the list a serious look-over.

"I can't believe anyone would eat a peanut butter cupcake, can you guys? BLECH!" I said.

"Not everyone objects to peanut butter, Tabs," said Kara. "Then again, most of us haven't slathered it in our hair." .

Pri looked confused. Of course, she didn't know about the jet tub incident. Actually, Kara's the only one besides my mom who knows about it. But it seemed like the right time to share an embarrassing story about myself.

By the time I got to the part about Mom's bloodcurdling scream when I chopped off my hair, Pri was laughing so hard she could barely breathe.

Things went pretty much back to normal between Pri and me after that.

GTG! I hear Mom's car pulling into the driveway. She'll accuse me of being rude if she finds my friends alone downstairs, even though they are perfectly FINE!

My prediction: When someone gets mad at you and lets you know it, and you can still get along afterward, you've stopped being project partners and started becoming friends.

My room / 7:30 p.m.

Sometimes my mom ROCKS! She's so happy to see us working on a fund-raiser for Maddie's school that she offered to treat Kara, Pri, and me to dinner at the Golden China Garden. (The General Tso's chicken was awesome, as usual.)

Know what was even more awesome? The four fortune cookies that came with our check! One look at them and I had a fabulous idea.

"Nobody touch the cookies!" I demanded.

Three sets of eyes looked at me as if I was crazy. And I guess I am, but still.

"Why not?" asked Pri.

"Because these cookies contain *fortunes* — ways to predict the future. Maybe one of THESE will point me to the right guy!"

I considered the positions of the cookies. It definitely matters what cookie ends up with which person. I mean, what if the fortune I got was actually meant for someone else?

The one closest to me seemed like the most obvious choice. I grabbed it and broke it open, before Kara and Pri picked up theirs. The fortune inside was absolutely perfect!

> A man will soon walk through
> the golden doorway of your life.

I looked over my shoulder at the entrance to Golden China Garden. Guess what color it was? Golden!

I pointed to the doors and handed the fortune to Kara. "The right guy should be walking through those doors any time now," I whispered to her.

At that point, Pri shrieked. "A-MAZE-ING!!!!!" She slapped her fortune down on the table.

> A business venture you are considering
> will come to fruition soon.

"Awesome. Cupcakes 4 Catastrophes is ready to go!" I cheered. Pri and I beamed at each other.

"Hmph," said Kara. "It was already going to come to fruition because we're being proactive about it. The fortune cookie has nothing to do with it."

"Oh yes, it does," I said. "This is a sign that we're on the right track! I, for one, believe in these predictions."

Kara snorted with laughter. "Then I guess you'll agree that your Mr. Right just stepped through the golden doorway."

"It's Mr. Rinehart from the office," said Mom, waving awkwardly. I wanted to put my fortune right in her hand, but I didn't think she'd be amused by that.

"Is that his son?" I asked.

Mom shook her head. "That must be the nephew he talks about. He's single and doesn't have any children."

"He's single!" Kara hooted. But she was laughing so hard it sounded like *Hehehehesssssingle*.

I reached over and snatched the fortune cookie from her hand while her reflexes were still dulled by laughter. I shoved a piece of it in my mouth before Kara could get it back. (If you don't eat at least a little bit of the cookie, the fortune doesn't count.) Then I read the fortune.

> A man will soon walk through the golden doorway of your life.

It was the same dang fortune! "You can have Mr. Rinehart," I said to Kara. "I'll take whoever comes next."

But the next person to walk through the golden doorway was definitely off-limits for me.

Chip Tyler! Unbelievable! Kara jumped up and went to give Chip a hug. "Guess it was my fortune after all," she said to me over her shoulder.

Well, there was one more cookie to try. Or so I thought. I went to reach for it, but Mom was popping it into her mouth. "What'd the fortune say?" I asked, hoping THAT one was meant for me.

She winked at me and stuffed the slip of paper into her wallet. GRRRRRR!

Mom shot down my suggestion to buy more cookies. That shows you how much she cares about my future!

My prediction: There are a lot of golden doorways out there, so there's still a chance that *the one* for me will walk through one of them.

My room / 9:00 p.m.

It's weird how you can be happy and excited about one part of your life, but frustrated and angry with another part.

See, I'm stoked about Cupcakes 4 Catastrophes, but my search for *the one* isn't going well at all.

I opened up my bedroom window and looked up at the sky. I considered picking another star to wish on, but that hadn't gotten me anywhere so far. Instead, I tried a more authoritative approach.

"Hey!" I called to the universe, "I need a little more guidance here! You put the pizza cheese guy in my path and you gave me a golden doorway. Now lead me to *the one*! Send me a sign!"

And the universe answered.

Or maybe it was just a car alarm.

Last night as I nestled all snug in my bed,
visions of cupcakes danced in my head.

Actually, it was more like visions of dancing cupcakes invaded my brain. Anyway, the point is that those dang cupcakes were trying to out-cute each other in an effort to get my attention. I guess this was a sign that Kara, Pri, and I should go ahead and choose the flavors C4C should offer. But how were we supposed to know which flavors to pick?

This morning I stumbled downstairs feeling bleary-eyed. I asked Mom how she'd choose which cupcake flavors to offer.

Luckily, she had some pretty good advice. "Think about your audience, Tabbi," she said. "Who is going to buy these cupcakes?"

The woman had a point! After all, 99.99999999999999999 percent of our customers would be middle school students. We needed to find out what flavors *they'd* like and start from there. Using the list Pri found on the Internet, I had just enough time before the Uncool Carpool arrived to make a survey and print out twenty-five copies.

What's your FAV FLAV? Feast your eyeballs on the flavors below, then put a 1 by your favorite cupcake flavor, a 2 by your second favorite, and a 3 by your third. Have a fav flav not listed? Give it a shout-out by writing it in the blank next to "Other." Thanks!

_____ 1. Vanilla
_____ 2. Pumpkin
_____ 3. Banana
_____ 4. Coffee
_____ 5. Chocolate
_____ 6. Lemon
_____ 7. Carrot
_____ 8. Red Velvet
_____ 9. Chocolate with Vanilla Icing
_____ 10. Peanut Butter
_____ 11. Strawberry
_____ 12. Chocolate Chip

Other: _____

Family room / 3:45

Kara, Pri, and I spent most of lunch tallying the FAV FLAV surveys we'd passed out at the beginning of the period. It was easy to see what the top flavors were: vanilla, chocolate, chocolate with vanilla icing, peanut butter (I can't BELIEVE peanut butter made the top six!), strawberry, and red velvet. Sure, chocolate had a few more votes than the others, but it didn't seem like a good idea to only offer chocolate cupcakes. Some people don't like chocolate, and some who do still wouldn't want it *every day*. We'd be losing out on potential sales if we only offered one flavor. But how could we tell which combination of these six flavors would actually sell best?

"Let's bring in two flavors a day for three days," Kara suggested. "We'll record which one sells best each day. Then we'll have a good idea which flavors are the most popular with our classmates. Those will have the greatest probability of selling best, therefore making the most money for Cupcakes 4 Catastrophes."

As soon as she said the word *probability*, Pri and I looked at each other. She was definitely thinking what I was thinking. This was confirmed .00000000000001 second later, when we actually said the exact same thing.

"Our probability project!!!!!!"

Predicting which cupcake flavor would be the most popular (chocolate!) was not complicated enough for an algebra project. But predicting which *combination* of flavors would best meet the demands of our classmates (and make us the most money in sales) was a lot more complex. I think it might work!

After lunch, we dropped by Mr. Gheary's room and added our note card to the bulletin board. Whew! I'm so glad we came up with something!

We will predict which combination of cupcake flavors best meets the demands of our classmates.

Tabitha and Priyanka

Thursday, September 20
My room / 3:59 p.m.

I'm getting very excited about Dianna's party tomorrow night. Everyone will be there — from the most popular kids to in-between-y kids like me and Kara. And not just because Dianna's parents make her include everyone.

If I'm lucky, the cute soccer boy will be there. Then I can just walk right up to him and ask his age. (Or get Kara to do it for me!) But even if he isn't, this will be the perfect opportunity to do more research for my probability project — the unofficial boyfriend-finding one — since a whole bunch of kids my age will all be together in one place.

I mean, the Faceplace survey Kara set up was good and all, but it hadn't gotten me any closer to finding a boyfriend. Probably because all of the questions we included, now that I think about it, had to do with getting the attention of a *particular* guy. So you kinda have to know *which* guy's attention you want for any of those suggestions (like communicating through texts, touching his arm, or messaging him through Faceplace) to work.

Obviously, I have NO IDEA who *the one* might be. So I needed more information that might lead me to actually *find him*. It seemed like getting answers to a few more questions would really help. Questions like:

- Is he likely to attend my school, or go somewhere else?
- Where should I hang out to give myself the greatest probability of meeting him? The gym? The cafeteria? Where?
- Is he more likely to be my age, older, or younger?

If I could find out the answers to these questions, I might actually be able to use the data from the Faceplace surveys to increase my probability of finding a boyfriend.

Now I just have to figure out how I can get this information from Dianna's party guests without being obvious. I mean, if I start quizzing people about their love lives and writing down their answers, I'll be avoided like a pile of fresh dog poop!

My room / 8:59 p.m.

Got it!!!! Got it! Got it! Got it! A brilliant, sneaky way to gather information while making your friends think they're playing a game. I called Kara right away to tell her my idea.

Our conversation pretty much went like this:

Me: You say party. I say bingo.

Kara: Party!

Me: Bingo!

Kara: Party!

Me: Bingo!

Kara: Party!

Me: Bingo! Party Bingo!

Kara: Okay, Tabs . . . what's this about?

Me: Remember at Camp Luna Moth when we played Party Bingo to get to know each other better?

Kara: Yeahhhhhhhhh . . .

Me: Well, those Party Bingo cards are just grids with different information like "I have blue eyes" in each square, remember?

Kara: Yeahhhhhhhh . . .

Me: And people walk around putting their initials in the squares that apply to them, right?

Kara: Yeahhhhhhhh . . .

Me: I'm thinking I can totally create a Party Bingo card with statements that allow me to gather information about people's crushes. Then I can use the info I get to increase the probability of actually finding a boyfriend.

Kara: You lost me.

Me: Never mind. You'll see tomorrow night. I've gotta call Dianna.

Kara: Sounds good. And Tabs?

Me: Yeah?

Kara: Party?

Me: BINGO!

When I called Dianna and offered to be in charge of a party game, she was like, "Well, I don't know. . . ."

So I offered to bring *three fabulous prizes.*

I have NO IDEA what kind of prizes I'll come up with, but I have lots of ideas about what kind of things to put on the Party Bingo Game boards.

PARTY BINGO

Directions: Party Bingo is a fun game to help you mingle and get to know your friends better. To play, get your pals to initial ONE box where the statement is true of them. Only one set of initials per box! To win a fabulous prize, be one of the first three people to get initials in all thirty squares.

I'm available.	I'm taken.	I met my crush at school.	I met my crush at a club meeting.	My older sister or brother thinks they are better than they actually are.
I met my crush in the library.	I love to read.	I've never met a cupcake I didn't like.	I have two or more pet dogs.	I met my crush in class.
My crush goes to my school, but I met him/her somewhere else.	I met my crush in the hallway.	I am musically talented.	I was attracted to my crush by the way he/she dresses.	I've been told I wear too much makeup.
I love cats.	I met my crush in the gym.	My favorite subject is lunch.	I met my crush at a sporting event.	I love pizza!
My crush is younger than me.	My mom still packs my lunch for me.	My crush is older than I am.	I've been to a concert.	I have ridden an elephant.
I sleep with a stuffed animal.	My crush is the same age I am.	I'm the master of *Just Dance*!	My crush goes to another school.	I met my crush in the cafeteria.

126

In order for this to work, I'll need to stand at the door with a clipboard. As guests arrive, I'll have them initial *all* squares that apply to them. I'll tell them I'm creating a key for the game. This way, I'll get info from everyone there.

Do they *have* to know you don't actually *need* a key for Party Bingo? I DON'T THINK SO.

Then I'll hand each kid a bingo card when it's time to start the game. I've already made sixty copies. Ready to go!

Friday, September 21
My completely ransacked room / 10:10 p.m.

About an hour before the party I had my own personal freak-out festival (the bad kind). I mean, so many things could go wrong with my plan that it suddenly felt like I was organizing a great big DISASTER!

The first thing I panicked about was pens. What if no one brought them? It'd completely ruin the game! I ran to Mom's desk and opened her office-supply drawer. She has tons of pens and pencils that she got for something like one cent a bag during the Staples back-to-school sale. I dug down to the bottom of the drawer and pulled out a pack.

I put the pens with the Party Bingo cards and looked over the instructions one more time. Two words that *should have* leapt out at me a couple of hours ago (when I had time to do something about it) suddenly jumped out at me now.

FABULOUS PRIZES

Oh great. Oh great, great, great, great, great. (When I say *great* here, I do not mean great in the good way, but in the bad, terrible, awful, *what have I done* kind of way.)

Kara and her dad would be here to pick me up in ten minutes and I had COMPLETELY forgotten about the prizes. I had no choice: I was going to have to bring something I already owned. This meant nothing would be fabulous, because I don't own anything fab except the UGGS my grandmom gave me last year for my birthday, and no one wants to win a pair of scuff-toed boots.

So I basically ransacked my own bedroom. I found out I'm pretty good at ransacking. Too bad it's not exactly a skill that leads to a reputable career.

How to ransack a room:
1. Dump every drawer onto the floor.
2. Open closet, pull out everything that isn't nailed in.
3. Use broom to push stuff out from under bed.
4. Pour contents from decorative baskets onto bed.

5. Using flailing hands and feet, shift through it
   all, looking for loot.

Unfortunately, my ransacking didn't get me too much. I mean, if I'd been a pirate, I'd have given up pirating right then and there. It was pitiful plunder.

I guess I'm thinking of pirates because one of the things I found was an unused stick-on fake mustache from my friend Phillip Bernard's birthday party a couple of years ago. That was back when we used to have girl-boy parties. Then we stopped those for a few years. But now the girl-boy parties are back. THANK GOODNESS!

In the end, the only things I found that could pass for prizes were three golden dollars from the tooth fairy and a tiny clip-on radio Uncle Mike sent me for my eleventh birthday. The radio didn't really work, but it was still in the box and it *looked* brand-new. Like a prize. A fabulous prize. With any luck, the winner wouldn't figure out it was broken until after the party.

After closing the door to my ransacked room, I went downstairs to Mom's desk and plundered through her office-supply drawer again, desperately looking for more loot. I found a pack of colored markers. I give them a D-minus as a party prize, but they were still a prize.

About then, Kara's dad pulled up. I ran to the kitchen to hug Mom good-bye.

She looked at my super-cute lavender sleeveless shirt and said, "It's chilly out. You need a sweater."

"I'm *fine*," I said. "Mr. McAllister's already here. I don't want to make him wait."

"Go tell him you'll be ready in a minute," said Mom. "I'll run up and get you a hoodie."

No way could I let that happen! Mom could NOT see my ransacked room. "I'm fine, Mom, fine. Hot even! Sweating already, see?" I swiped a hand across my forehead, wiping away fake sweat as I backed toward the door.

Mom advanced on me and the stairs. "It'll only take a second. . . ." she started, but I was out the door, charging for the car before she hit the bottom step.

I got in, slammed the door behind me, and cried, "Step on it!"

Mr. McAllister and Kara looked at me like I was crazy. (Yeah, I get that a lot.) But things were going to get a whole lot crazier if we didn't make like a tree and LEAVE before my neat-freak mom's eyeballs made contact with my room.

"Um . . . ready to go," I added as calmly as possible. As Mr. McAllister pulled out of our driveway, I saw my room light flip on. Even if I had no imagination whatsoever, I'd still be able to picture what my mom's face looked like at that second.

If Mom weren't so . . . so . . . *Mom*, she'd have known not to worry — that I'd clean it all back up. Just not before the party.

(I'm sure she wasn't happy when she dialed my cell to yell at me and heard it ring right there in my room . . . but I'd decided not to bring it along. Wouldn't want to lose it or anything.)

Anyway, Mom was on the phone with Uncle Mike when I got home. I'd barely gotten the toes of my boots through the doorway when she shoved this into my hands:

Go straight to your room and start cleaning! We'll have a chat as soon as I get off the phone!!!!!!

So I came up here and started throwing clothes into my drawers and closet. Then I thought I'd better drag out this journal and record as much as I can before Mom gets up here. Who knows when I'm ever going to have free time again.

Anyway, as long as they're still talking, let me get to what happened at the party. As soon as we got there, I stationed myself at the door with clipboard, pens, and my Party Bingo cards. I made sure everyone who entered initialed the squares for my "key." (Only one or two kids grumbled about it; most just scribbled down their initials as quickly as they could, since I was basically the gatekeeper to the party, and they wanted to hurry up and get inside.)

Then we played the game, which really did make people mingle. It looked like everyone was having fun. No one suspected my ulterior motive! It all went perfectly . . . until people actually started winning.

The Vine won the mini radio, which I gave her after pretending to check her bingo card against the "key." I was glad she won it because she was too busy hanging all over Malcolm (grrrr) to figure out it didn't work. Then Kara won the markers, which was a HUGE relief because she actually likes markers. Plus, she helped me out by making a big deal of how great they were. I held my breath and waited to give out the last prize.

By that time, I was wishing we were all back in kindergarten. Back then, three golden dollars would have been an AWESOME prize. But eventually you get old enough to realize that people who want you to believe golden dollars are "special" are keeping some pretty crucial math from you.

One Golden Dollar = One Tattered Paper Dollar

And once you can figure that out, they don't seem so cool anymore.

I just hoped whoever won them was a guy. A boy would probably pocket 'em without saying something sarcastic like *Gee, thanks, three whole dollars.*

But of course, the worst possible person won.

"Ta-da! Done!" shouted Maybelline.

I reached into my bag to pull out the money, but it wasn't there. Not in the front pocket, not in the back pocket, not in the main compartment. Not anywhere! Cra-Z!

I frantically searched my pants pockets but only found that stupid stick-on mustache.

"Well," said Maybelline, holding out her hand, "I played your lame game, now give me my fabulous prize!"

Really, there was only one thing I could do.

"HERE YOU GO!"

I handed over the mustache.

"Ewww!" Maybelline dropped the 'stache. Everyone in the room kinda took a step back.

I admit, the hairy, black, wrinkled-up mustache didn't look so great, but what'd they think it was? A tarantula?

Maybe they just want to distance themselves because of the wrath of Maybelline. It has a fear factor equal to that of the world's biggest spider.

"That's the worst prize I've ever seen!" said The Sponge. (Her real name is Tiffany Davidson, but Kara and I call her The Sponge because she soaks up everything she can about Maybelline.)

It looked like my social life would soon be as lifeless as the fake mustache.

Then Alex B saved the day. "Hey, Phillip," he called. "Didn't you have mustaches like this at your third-grade birthday party?"

I was thinking *Um . . . exactly like those.* I swear I crossed my fingers, my toes, and my eyes, hoping no one else would realize the mustache on the floor was actually a pirate party favor. Despite my super-cute sleeveless top and lack of hoodie, I started sweating for real. It looked like there was only one word for my current situation: *BUSTED!*

"I remember those." Alex laughed. He picked up the mustache and stuck it on. It wiggled on his lip as he chewed his gum. Then he turned to Maybelline and asked, "Ever kissed a dude with a mustache?"

Let's just say she has . . . now.

Suddenly the room filled with cheers, making Maybelline the center of attention again, which would normally annoy me. But I was okay with it since it took the attention off of me and my sorry prize. Then Dianna's parents responded to the cheering by running in and breaking everything up. Everyone was so distracted after that, the whole thing blew over. Whew!

Know what's unbelievable? Alex B wore that dang mustache for the *rest of the night*, making it the *coolest* prize instead of the *lamest*. It must be awesome to have that kind of social superpower: the ability to turn something lame into something cool just by wearing it. I know girls who would *kill* for that particular power.

Seriously, I couldn't tell you how many mouths this exact sentence came out of:

"Hey, Tabbi, got any more of those mustaches?"

Alex B is so cute and nice. Sighhhhh. And he SAVED me from complete disaster. Why does he have to have such bad taste in girls?

My prediction: Someday Alex B will see the light. When he does, I'll be basking in its glow, ready for him to notice me!

GTG: Sounds like Mom is winding up her convo with Uncle Mike.

My slightly less messy room / 11:30 p.m.

'Twas the night of the party and all through the house
  Not a creature was stirring, not even my mom.
So basically that means it's safe for me to write again!

After Mom got off of the phone, and AFTER I listened to her rant and rave about the state of my room, and AFTER I put away everything I'd dumped on my bed, and AFTER I could tell Mom was asleep, I looked at my Party Bingo "key" and compiled my results. I couldn't stand to wait until morning to see what my research predicted.

I got fifty-seven responses!

Forty-two of these said they were taken, so that's the number I started with. Ten were taken by each other, so I had to pick whether to use Maybelline's answers or Alex B's, for example, since obviously they "met their crush" in the same place.

This meant I ended up with thirty-seven responses. I divided the information into three categories, then went to this website called Pie Charts and Candy Bar Graphs where you upload your data and it creates a . . . um . . . tasty-looking graph or chart.

Party Bingo Data: PLACE
Met at School vs. Met Somewhere Else

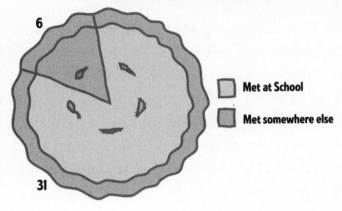

6

31

Met at School

Met somewhere else

And you know when it comes to pie, always aim for the biggest piece! So you can see that my chances of meeting *the one* are much greater at school than anywhere else.

I'm not too disappointed by this info because I already know that cute soccer boy goes to my school. Bonus! He wasn't at the party, but maybe the rest of the results will give me a clue about how or where to meet him!

Oof! Just heard a toilet flush. Guess Mom is up and about.

My prediction: I'll find out a lot more about how to increase my chances of finding a boyfriend tomorrow.

Saturday, September 22
My ~~room~~ prison. Ugh. / 10:48 a.m.

I'm just taking a quick break from cleaning my room. I don't think I can stand to fold another pair of socks or put away another bottle of nail polish. I mean, it seems scientifically IMPOSSIBLE that while it takes something like forty-five seconds to ransack a room, it takes three whole hours to clean it back up!

Mom says I can't leave until it is "spotless . . . cleaner than before . . ." which I'm sure it will be, because I found a *ton* of junk I don't need anymore that I threw away.

Drawers – Old Junk = More Room in My Room

You never know what you're going to find when you dump out a drawer! I mean, I found gum that was so gooey and gross that I wouldn't put it in my mouth EVEN if I'd just wolfed down an order of onion rings and then found out my crush was about to ask me out. It was that disgusting! (Okay: I totally *would* put a gross piece of gum in my mouth before blasting my crush with nasty onion breath.)

But I also found something that might be extremely valuable in making predictions. Something that I already own, but had completely forgotten about.

A Magic 8 Ball!

It'd been a long time since I'd sought the wisdom of the 8 Ball. I picked up the plastic sphere and looked down at the number 8 on top of it. "Will I find a boyfriend this year?" I whispered. I turned the ball over in my hands and watched as the white letters appeared in the blue ink.

At least it wasn't a no! I wasn't sure whether or not to try again right away . . . or to wait. But if I did wait, how long? Would I see the answer I wanted if I waited thirty minutes, or did I need to wait a few days before trying again?

Waiting was too much trouble!

"Will I find a boyfriend this year?" I asked again and gave it another shake.

Grrr. Grrr. Grrr. I WAS concentrating! But okay. I took a deep breath and tried to clear my mind of everything but the mysteries of the 8 Ball. I closed my eyes. I spoke each word super clearly so the dumb thing would understand exactly what I was asking.

"Will. I. Find. A. Boyfriend. This. Year?" I jiggled the ball before flipping it over.

What???? This thing reminds me of a kindergartner saying, *I know a secret and you do-ooo naaaah-ot.*

I spoke to the 8 Ball one last time. "You might be an 8 Ball, but you're about to go bowling!"

As I watched it roll back under my bed, I became more convinced than ever that if I want the future predicted, I'm gonna have to rely on something more dependable. Like algebra. It was time for me to get back to my boyfriend-finding probability project and finish recording the information I gathered from Party Bingo.

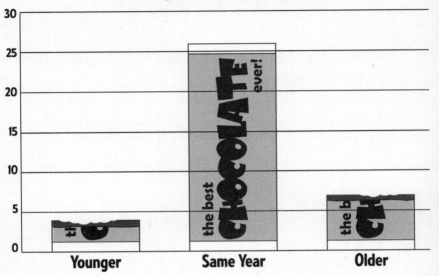

Party Bingo Data: AGE
Younger vs. Same Age vs. Older

You can see for yourself how this stacks up on the candy bar graph! Clearly, I need to be looking for someone *my same age*. But where will I find him? No worries, that's covered in the next set of data!

Party Bingo Data: EXACT SCHOOL LOCATION
Cafeteria vs. Class vs. Library vs. Hallway vs. Gym
vs. School Sports vs. Club Meeting

Cafeteria	🍬🍬🍬🍬🍬🍬🍬🍬🍬
Class	🍬🍬🍬🍬🍬🍬🍬
Library	🍬🍬
Hallway	
Gym	🍬🍬🍬🍬
Sports	🍬🍬🍬🍬🍬🍬
Club	🍬🍬🍬

🍬 = one person

So I have an okay chance of meeting *the one* at school (anywhere but a hallway), but I have the *greatest probability* of meeting him in the cafeteria. Makes sense. It's where we all come together.

After looking at the Party Bingo data, I'm prepared to make the following prediction: I will meet my future boyfriend at school, in the cafeteria, and he will be my age.

I thought about the different boys my age at school. Suddenly, I realized I already knew one of them who fit *all three categories*. I distinctly remember the day I first met him . . .

in the cafeteria when he asked me to trade my chocolate milk for his plain milk. Even back then, he was so cute that I didn't think twice about the trade! So what if we were in elementary school? It still counts.

When I thought about how nice he was at the party last night — basically saving me from social isolation and all — I had to call Kara. . . .

Me: Alex B is such a nice person.

Kara (groaning): Tabs, not again.

Me: He is! I can't help it. I never really stopped liking him.

Kara: *Really?* You still liked Alex when you were dating Evan? And James?

Me: Well, not as much. But, yeah. He's so perfect.

Kara: No. He's not. He humiliated his girlfriend last year.

Me: She deserved it.

Kara: Still, it makes me wonder how nice he really is.

Me: I'm pretty sure he's only with Maybelline until he finds the right girl.

Kara: Maybe.

Me: And I'm the right girl.

Kara: Come *on!*

Me: No, seriously. I compiled the results of the Party Bingo survey, and he fits all categories. He's my age, he goes to my school, and we met in the cafeteria.

Kara: Lots of guys fall into those categories.

Me: But none of the rest of them saved me by wearing a fake mustache all night.

Kara: I don't think he did that for *you*, Tabs.

Me: Gotta go.

Kara will never see Alex for who he truly is: a super-nice, super-cute, super-perfect guy waiting to be discovered by the right girl: ME!

Sunday, September 23
My super-clean room (If you don't look under the bed!) / 6:31 p.m.

3 Girls + Afternoon Baking = 24 Perfect Cupcakes

I'd say that sums up my day pretty well. Can't wait to start raising money to help my cousin's school!

My prediction: We're going to exceed our six-hundred-dollar goal!

Monday, September 24
Family room / 8:00 p.m.

We set up a table right next to the drink machine in the cafeteria so when people came to buy drinks, they might change their minds and spend their money on cupcakes instead. Our first customer was Chip. Kara's so lucky! He's such a supportive boyfriend. When he came to our table, he said (loudly), "These cupcakes look so delicious. I'll take one of each!"

We did pretty well for our first day. I *thought* we did, anyway, until Kara explained the math.

She handed me this note card.

Cupcakes 4 Catastrophes   9/24
Total Merchandise: 24 cupcakes (12 Vanilla, 12 Chocolate)
Price: $1.00 each   Goal: 600 cupcakes

#Vanilla Sold: 4
Chocolate Sold: 5
Total Sold: 9 ($9.00)

Total Needed: $600.00
Sales so Far: $9.00
To Go: $591.00

"The good news is we made nine dollars," she said. "The bad news is that we have to sell nine cupcakes per day for the next sixty-five-point-six days to make our goal."

"No problem," said Pri. "We have thirty-two days between today and October twenty-sixth. We'll sell more and more cupcakes when the word starts spreading about how delicious they are."

"Thirty-two days includes Saturdays and Sundays," said Kara, frowning.

I looked at my calendar. There were eight weekend days between now and October twenty-sixth. This only left us *twenty-four* days to sell *sixty-five-point-six* days' worth of cupcakes. Ugh.

Kara punched at her calculator. "This is a big problem. We needed to sell all two dozen cupcakes every single day between now and October twenty-sixth to make six hundred dollars. And that includes today."

"Still," I said, "we'll be really really close to our goal if we can sell out for the next twenty-four school days."

"And maybe some days we can even sell something like three dozen cupcakes," added Pri. "Then we'll exceed our goal. We can do it!"

"Don't cheer yet," said Kara. "We might sell fewer cupcakes tomorrow. Then it'll be even harder to meet our goal."

"Think positive," I said. "We'll sell more cupcakes!"

"More cupcakes!" cheered Pri.

"Let's do it," said Kara, but she didn't look completely convinced we'd be able to.

Oh, and I almost forgot to mention the best part. Alex Brantley bought *two* cupcakes! And when I handed them to him, he said, "Thanks, Tabbi!" and winked at me!!!

So what if he gave one of the two cupcakes to Maybelline?

*Note to future self: When Alex B starts dating you, remember that he likes chocolate cupcakes.

Tuesday, September 25
Uncool Carpool / 3:01 p.m.

Kara says I'm crazy, but I swear Alex B is flirting with me.

"Tabs," she said, "I'm pretty sure he has a crush on the cupcakes, not you." Rude!

But I think she's wrong. I mean, he didn't *have* to buy two cupcakes again today. And yeah, he did give one to Maybelline again. But still.

I decided it was time to start recording data about Alex, and maybe other guys I'm interested in, too. I created a chart using the two sets of data I'd already collected:

Party Bingo data: predicts WHERE I am most likely to meet my future boyfriend and HOW old he will be.

Faceplace data: indicates WHAT I need to do to get his attention. (I used the top answer from each category.)

Boy Prediction Checklist				
	♥	Alex B	?	?
Party Bingo Data	Goes to My School	✓		
	Met in Cafeteria	✓		
	Is My Age	✓		
Faceplace Data (How to get his attention.)	Texting			
	Touching Arm or Hand			

The more boxes I check off, the easier it will be to predict WHO my next boyfriend will be. I already have the first three columns checked off for Alex B! So now I need to work on getting him to notice me. You know, just in case he and Maybelline ever break up. And hopefully it won't be long before I can replace those question marks with other guys' names!

Oh! I have other good news to share! Cupcakes 4 Catastrophes did better today than yesterday. Our biz is growing!

Cupcakes 4 Catastrophes   9/25
Total Merchandise: 24 cupcakes (12 Red Velvet, 12 PB)
Price: $1.00 each   Goal: 600 cupcakes

Red Velvet Sold: 11
Peanut Butter Sold: 10
Total Sold: Almost two dozen! ($21.00)

Total Needed: $600.00
Sales so far: $30
To Go: $570

Wednesday, September 26
My room / 8:23 p.m.

At lunch today, we ran into a mathematical problem:

Usual Selling Spot + Someone Else's Table
= Intruder in Our Territory

I mean, I *know* I don't own the cafeteria. DUH! But I *don't appreciate* anyone making an announcement to that effect as if it were some up-to-date newsflash! Especially if that *anyone* is a particular *someone* who wears too much *makeup* and dates a guy who is *too good for her*! Maybelline!

Basically, we were forced to relocate Cupcakes 4 Catastrophes because Maybelline was setting up a table next to the drink machine. We picked a spot near the windows and got busy setting out cupcakes.

Then Pri gasped. She was pointing across the cafeteria. "She can't do that!"

Kara's lips were pressed together as tightly as two halves of a clamshell. When she opened them a moment later, she said, "Maybelline tends to be able to do anything she wants."

"Oh yeah?" said Pri. Then she marched her tiny little self right over to Maybelline's table. Before we knew it, she was having a full-blown conversation with our rival.

"If she knew Maybelline the way we do, she wouldn't bother," I whispered to Kara. She nodded. We watched as Pri and Maybelline talked.

Pri came charging back to our table, looking as angry as a miniature bull.

"Apparently," she huffed, "she has *permission!*"

The three of us watched as Maybelline and The Sponge began unpacking plastic containers, their mouths curved in self-satisfied smiles. Cupcakes, cupcakes, cupcakes in all three boxes!!!!

"I'm going to throw this away," said Kara, balling up a perfectly clean napkin and heading for the trashcan that stood a few paces from Maybelline's table.

She was back a few seconds later, smiling reassuringly. "No worries, Tabs," she said. "Her cupcakes look like they're made from a mix, and the icing is flat. They're nowhere *near* as appetizing as ours."

Know what? I was worried anyway. So far today we'd sold four cupcakes. All to returning customers. If we were going to raise enough money for Cupcakes 4 Catastrophes, we needed to sell a little more than twenty-four a day. Which meant we needed new customers *in addition* to our returning ones.

"Five," said Pri suddenly.

"What are you talking about?" asked Kara.

"They've sold five cupcakes. That's one more than we have."

A line was starting to form at the enemy camp. A short line, but long in comparison to the line at our table. The line that wasn't.

Maybelline's first customers were her usual crew. Alex L, who was still dating The Sponge, Dylan Hudson, and — it makes me particularly sad to say this — Alex Brantley. He bought two of hers and none of mine. ☹

I did see him glance longingly toward our table, though. I elbowed Kara. "Look, there's hope for me and Alex B. He might be in her line, but he's looking over here."

"Yeah," said Kara, "but he's only checking out the cupcakes."

I studied Alex's face. Kara was right. He was definitely eyeing the strawberry cupcakes. I hate it when Kara's right!

"I wish I were a strawberry cupcake," I sighed.

"Eww," said Kara.

Other people in Maybelline's line included the hangers-on. You know, the people who always gush over Maybelline but aren't actually in her group. People like The Vine. Then there were the ones who just wanted what everyone else had.

Even if what they had was a cupcake inferior in looks and taste. People can be so dumb!

I picked up a strawberry cupcake in a silver foil liner and held it up. The icing was a perfect swirl of pale pink. A fresh strawberry sat on top of it. It was a work of art, if I do say so myself. "Look at this cupcake! Can you believe ANYONE would buy one of those ugly things instead?" I gestured to Maybelline's table.

"No!" said Pri. "I *can't* believe it!" She stood up, fully displaying her chartreuse *Love Thy Cupcake* T-shirt with pink cupcakes on the front. "Look at this beautiful cupcake!" Pri yelled to the cafeteria. Everyone looked. No one purchased. It was not a great moment for Cupcakes 4 Catastrophes.

Pri's face fell. She smiled apologetically. "It was worth a shot."

"No, it wasn't!" cried Kara. "Now our humiliation is more public than ever. Thanks a lot." (Right here, *thanks a lot* actually means the exact opposite of *thanks a lot*.)

Probably, if I called Kara right now, she'd tell me that she regretted making that statement. Because what happened next was a whole lot more humiliating . . . to HER.

See, Chip walked in about then. His eyes darted over to where our table had been set up for the past two days. Kara waved at him from our new location, but he obviously didn't see her. If he had, he wouldn't have done what he did next, which was to get in Maybelline's line.

"I can't believe that jerk!" said Kara.

"He didn't see you," said Pri.

"So what!" snapped Kara. "He knows how I feel about Maybelline! I think he's actually about to buy a cupcake from her! It's the ultimate betrayal!"

I wasn't too happy about Chip's support of Maybelline, but Kara was overreacting. I mean, she obviously hasn't had a boy celebrate a two-week anniversary with her in the morning, then have that same boy break up with her two hours later because of Maybelline. Now *that's* the ultimate betrayal.

"I'll stop him before he gives her money!" claimed Pri. Quick as lightning, she was out of her seat.

Kara's arm flashed out and barred her way. "Don't bother. He isn't my boyfriend. Let him eat cupcake."

"I thought you were dating Chip," said Pri. She can be so clueless sometimes!

"I was. Until about five seconds ago."

"Kara . . . you know he wouldn't be over there if he'd seen you over here," I said.

"So?" Kara flipped her hair in a way that reminded me of her sister, Julie. "I don't want to be with someone who buys cupcakes behind my back."

Chip was paying Maybelline now. He turned around. Looking down at the cupcake, he peeled off the plain paper wrapper, then stuffed the entire cake in his mouth at once. Nice — not!

"Priyanka," said Kara. "Can you make that announcement again? Right now? The one about the beautiful cupcake?"

Pri looked confused. "I thought you didn't like it when I did that."

"Just do it!" growled Kara.

So Priyanka stood on a chair, holding a strawberry cupcake up like Lady Liberty's torch, and made the exact same *look at this beautiful cupcake* announcement.

Chip's head jerked up. His brown eyes flew open in surprise. Or maybe it was horror. Kara was looking at him, too, but this time she wasn't waving. Her arms were too busy being crossed over her chest.

Chip hurried over to our table, looking worried. His jaws were chewing as fast as they could, in a completely futile attempt to destroy the evidence, even though he knew he'd been caught red-handed.

"Hi, Chip," said Kara coolly. "What's up?"

"Ummm . . ." He looked like he was trying to think of something to say to cover the fact that his mouth was full of enemy cupcake. But he must have seen the same *don't even try it* expression on Kara's face that I did.

"I just wanted to check out the competition," said Chip, his cheeks full of overprocessed cupcake made from a mix. Some chocolate cupcake spilled out of his mouth and crumbs alighted on the front of his red shirt, like flies.

Kara looked like she wanted to throw up, but I don't think

it was because of Chip's poor eating skills. "Well. How was the competition?" she asked.

"Terrible," said Chip. "They're awful. Thought you'd wanna know." He was smiling sheepishly at Kara, who was not smiling back. At all.

"Buy one of ours, then, to get that terrible taste out of your mouth," Pri joked, trying to smooth things over. Her suggestion ended up having the opposite effect.

"Ummmm." Chip was looking down, shuffling his feet. "I can't right now. . . . I'm out of cash."

Nobody said anything. I kinda felt sorry for Chip. Kinda, but not enough to help him out.

"How about I buy one today and pay tomorrow?" he offered. "You take credit, right?"

That was the last straw for Kara. "Your credit is no good here!"

I know she didn't mean to, but she yelled it loud enough to make people turn around. It was kind of bad for our already bad business. But Kara didn't notice. By this time, she was flying across the cafeteria like a kite in a windstorm. As she left, she rushed by Jonah Nate's table so fast that she accidentally knocked his chocolate milk to the floor.

"Kaaaaraaaa!" he cried. But Kara's been blocking out Jonah Nate for so long that she didn't even hear him.

Chip turned to Pri and me. "What should I do?"

Pri surprised me by getting all sassy. "Go get advice from the girl who sold you that cupcake."

Chip turned around and walked away with slumped shoulders.

Pri didn't seem to notice. Her big brown-black eyes were already back to focusing on Maybelline. "Her boxes are empty," she said.

"Meaning?"

"She sold twenty-four, and we sold four." Pri sighed. "Her cupcakes don't even look like they taste good," she added. "So why are they selling, instead of ours?"

"Because she's not selling cupcakes," I said. "She's selling popularity."

It was so FRUSTRATING!

I started packing up cupcakes as fast as I could. The bell was gonna ring any minute now, and I didn't want Maybelline walking by and seeing my mountain of unsold cupcakes.

Thursday, September 27
Mr. Gheary's room / 9:40 a.m.

When I first got here, I thought Pri was absent. But I was wrong! Turns out my eyes were so used to seeing her in loud colors that I didn't notice her sitting quietly in a white T-shirt until I was close enough to read the black writing on the front. I couldn't help it — I busted out laughing.

HAND OVER THE CUPCAKES AND NO ONE GETS HURT

Perfect! Is it too much to hope that Maybelline heeds the warning?

Cafeteria / 12:30 p.m.

The good news: We sold all twenty-four cupcakes!

The bad news: Chip bought twenty of them!

The bad news for Chip: Kara didn't care. She sold all twenty with her nose in the air and her eyes focused on the ceiling above his head. Poor guy.

The really bad news as pointed out by Pri: "Maybelline's booth is wrecking our probability project. How can we know which flavors students prefer when they're buying her cupcakes instead of ours? Chip buying everything he can to get Kara back doesn't count. I'm pretty sure he's not thinking about flavors."

My prediction: We're in trouble.

While packing away the twenty — yes, twenty — cupcakes we still had on our hands at the end of lunch, I decided it was time to wave the white flag of surrender. I was sick of this. Sick of the humiliation. Sick of wasting time and money. Sick of worrying my cousin's school might not get the library it needed.

"I'm done!" I said. "We started a great project for a great cause, and that . . . that manicured Komodo dragon is ruining it all. I've baked my last cupcake!" When I said this, my voice was as quavery as Jell-O. ☹!

Then Pri said the weirdest thing: "Do you think because you are virtuous, that there shall be no more cakes?"

"Huh?" said Kara and I at the exact same time.

"Shakespeare," said Pri. "It's a quote."

"And you're quoting Shakespeare because . . ." said Kara.

"I think he meant the nice guy does not always win. But we can't give up! If we do, Five Corners Elementary won't get the money. And we'll fail our big algebra project."

"She's right," said Kara. "I say we don't give up. It's not your style, Tabs. Aren't you the girl who never backs down?"

Know what? I *am* that girl! We wouldn't back down. But something had to change. We needed a plan. A battle plan.

You know that white flag of surrender I mentioned

earlier? Well, I'm ripping it into strips and using it for bandages — the enemy is gonna need 'em to bandage up her pride!

My prediction: It's not over until we've raised six hundred dollars! (After that, Maybelline can sell all of the over-processed, made-from-a-mix cupcakes she wants.)

Band room (Substitute) / 1:45 p.m.

After lunch, I had these things tipping the balance on my scales of happiness:

- ☹ Having to take home uneaten cupcakes
- ☹ Realizing Alex B will never like me, unless I turn into a cupcake
- ☹ Knowing that Maybelline is outselling us with an inferior product
- ☹ Being so busy with cupcakes that I haven't had time to work on my more important project — the one that uses probability to help me predict how to find a boyfriend

Then something wonderful happened that tipped the scales right back where they should be. I was walking down the hall when I heard a cell phone blaring — it had a ring-tone like a fire alarm! Everyone knows to shut their ringers off before entering Spring Valley Middle because Principal O'Neal loves this equation:

$$\text{Cell Phone Noise} + \text{Principal O'Neal's Ear} = 1 \text{ Student} - 1 \text{ Phone}$$

I looked around to see whose cell was in danger. A cute, dark-haired guy was frantically pushing buttons to silence his phone.

As soon as I saw him, it was like my own personal alarm sounded (silently, in my brain). Remember when I asked the universe to lead me to *the one*? And then a CAR ALARM went off? Maybe THIS was the sign I've been looking for!

That cell phone alarm might be the universe's way to lead me to HIM.

There are some things in life that you *want to know*. Maybe you're curious about how something works, or where your friend got her super-cool purse.

Then there are other things you *really should know*. Like the material for tomorrow's test. Like your own address and phone number.

Then there are other things that you *urgently need to know*. Things your life could depend on. Like how to dial 911, and to never talk to strangers. Especially if the strangers are in a car and you're on foot and they ask you to come up to the window to look at a puppy.

There are some things that you *desperately want to know* and it feels like your life depends on knowing them, but it doesn't. These things seem even more important than the things you *actually* need to know. They are the burning questions that have you dialing your best friend over and over, even if you're 100 percent sure she's been grounded and doesn't even have her phone. The things that make you hurt, almost physically, until you find out the answers. Wanting to know sits like a heavy weight on your chest, taking your breath away right when you need it to do something like run down a crowded hallway just to have a chance to meet HIM.

HE was the cute soccer boy, the one I hadn't seen since Chip ruined my chance to find out more about him! And I *desperately wanted to know* where he was going. It would be the first step in finding out more about him! I wasn't going to lose sight of him this time.

I was about to sprint forward when Dylan Hudson stepped right in front of me and I totally lost sight of HIM. Sometimes I hate being short! I was forced to use my height, or lack of it, to my advantage. I ducked and darted. I scooted around my classmates and dipped under elbows. I jumped up and looked over the crowd to see if HE was still there.

Darn! Didn't see him. I jumped again. Yes! Bouncing

black curls were turning down D hall. Okay, I could deal with that.

A few seconds later I reached the intersection of the main hallway and D hall. Nothing. So I started strolling down the long hallway, casually looking into the narrow door windows. I saw all kinds of people I did *not* want to see — like James's new girlfriend, Kaitlin — but not even a peek of who I *did* want to see.

The hall was starting to clear out, which meant the bell would ring any second. Shoot! It was a lonnnnnnng walk from where I was, at the end of D hall, to Mrs. Ries's class on B hall. Even if I ran, I'd be tardy. But since

$$30 \text{ Seconds Late} = \text{Tardy}$$
$$\text{AND}$$
$$5 \text{ Minutes Late} = \text{Tardy}$$

I figured the following equation was also true, even though it doesn't make sense:
$$30 \text{ Seconds} = 5 \text{ Minutes}$$

So naturally, I didn't run, even when the bell started ringing. By my calculations, I still had at least four and a half minutes to get to class.

I glanced into Mrs. Hill's room. There was Pri! She must be in advanced English. She looked up, caught my eye, and started waving madly. Sometimes that girl is so clueless. I waved back quickly and hurried away before Mrs. Hill could come see what was distracting one of her students. Mrs. Hill isn't too fond of distractions.

Hooray! I spotted the curly black hair through the window of the very next door I passed. He was seated in the front row of advanced art. A good sign! Sixth graders aren't allowed to take that class, since you have to take introductory art first. I pulled the chart out of my pocket and updated it right then and there.

Boy Prediction Checklist			Alex B	Soccer Boy	?
		♥	Alex B	Soccer Boy	?
Party Bingo Data		Goes to My School	✓	✓	
		Met in Cafeteria	✓		
		Is My Age	✓	?	
Faceplace Data (How to get his attention.)		Texting			
		Touching Arm or Hand			

When I was the only one left in the hall, I headed back toward Mrs. Ries's room. I know I'll be tardy, but it was worth it! And who *cares* if I'm tardy?

(Late) Uncool Carpool / 4:31 p.m.

List of people who cared if I was tardy:

1. Mrs. Ries, who reminded me that it was my third tardy in a row, so I had to show up for after-school detention or be marked absent.
2. My discussion group, because they weren't allowed to start without me, and since we had to start late, we didn't complete our discussion form, so we all lost five points.
3. My mom, who nearly exploded when she got the phone call, because "People who are late for work get fired, and being tardy to class is no way to build a good work ethic!"
4. My neighbor Mrs. Winston, because Mom had to call her from work and ask her to make a special trip back to school to pick me up thirty minutes after dismissal time.
5. Me. Because everyone in my discussion group is mad at me.

Kara thought it'd be a good idea to visit the mall for inspiration for Cupcakes 4 Catastrophes. Her older sister, Julie, agreed to take us. On the way there, I told them about yesterday's sighting. I must have described him perfectly, because Kara said, "Oh yeah, I've seen that guy."

"You've seen him?" I said. "Where?"

"In the hall, like you," said Kara.

"Who IS he?" I asked. "He's so cute. Don't you love his dimples?"

"Dimples?" said Pri. "That must be Andres."

"You KNOW him?" I asked.

Pri nodded. "He rides my bus."

"Lucky," I said. "You get to see him every day. I've only seen him, like, three times in the hallway. Never at lunch or anything."

"I think he was in the cafeteria once or twice last week," said Kara. "But I don't remember seeing him at lunch before that."

"You didn't," said Pri. "Andres told me they keep readjusting his schedule. It just got changed, so now he has lunch when we do. I saw him in the cafeteria last week, too."

"Why didn't you guys tell me he was in the cafeteria?" I asked.

Pri and Kara looked at each other and smiled. Grrr.

"How were we supposed to know you liked Andres?" asked Kara.

"I don't like him," I said quickly. "I just think he's cute, that's all. Do you know what grade he's in?"

Pri shook her head. "Want me to ask him for you?"

I definitely DID NOT! No telling what Pri would say to him.

Julie's car pulled into the parking lot about then, so we went to the mall looking for ideas to improve cupcake sales. We didn't know what we were looking for, but we hoped we'd recognize it when we found it.

Luckily, it didn't take us long to recognize it! Because . . .

Malls = Tons of Stores = Lots of People
= Lots of Growling Stomachs = Food Courts
= Great Idea

Get it? Just in case you don't, I'll walk you through the process of how we came up with the BEST MARKETING PLAN EVER. Here's a clue: toothpicks.

Step 1: Go to a mall food court.
Step 2: Observe the lines at each restaurant.
Step 3: See the long line at the Bamboo Dragon Express.
Step 4: Observe the guy with chicken bits on a toothpick.

Step 5: Take a toothpick sample.

Step 6: Join crowd in line at Bamboo Dragon Express.

Our conversation as we dined on sesame chicken:

Kara: Are you guys thinking what I'm thinking?

Me: Absolutely.

Pri: What are you guys thinking?

Kara: Why we didn't we think of it before?

Me: I know, right?

Pri (looking at the guy handing out chicken samples): Oh! You think if we start giving out free samples —

Kara: We're bound to sell more cupcakes! Not that many kids even *tasted* ours. Maybelline stole most of our business after only two days.

Me: Once everyone has a chance to taste ours, I predict they'll buy from us instead of Maybelline!

At this point we did a three-way high five . . . which I guess equals something like a high fifteen.

Me: *Operation Get Our Business Back* starts Monday!

Pri: Maybe not Monday. (Whips out her phone and starts texting.)

Kara: Why not Monday?

Pri (looks at phone, which just beeped): First of all, let's let Maybelline think we quit. Then we can take her by surprise . . . and . . . well, I have a secret weapon . . . something that'll make a real statement. (Her phone beeped again.) But I can't get it until Tuesday. So can we start *Operation Get Our Business Back* on Wednesday? Please?

Me: What's the secret weapon?

Pri: It'll be better to show you than to tell you. Wednesday morning, okay?

Kara and I looked at each other and nodded. So far, Pri's ideas had been solid. We were going to have to trust her.

My prediction: Maybelline isn't going to know what hit her.

Monday, October 1
My room / 9:00 p.m. (Commonly known to people with normal parents as time to start watching that last TV show of the night.)

Not having cupcakes to sell today freed me up at lunch to try to find out more about Andres. I pulled out my chart, erased *Soccer Boy*, and replaced it with *Andres*.

I noticed he brought his own lunch, and that he sat with a group of other guys who brought lunch from home. I was hoping to find a way to meet him, but I chickened out. Toward the end of lunch, however, I made it a point to walk by him and smile. He smiled back!

BUT

(Why does there always have to be a big ol' *but* right in the middle of things, messing them up?)

I might have completely ruined my chances with him after school. It's kinda Pri's fault. See, she was standing in the bus line next to him and she saw me walking toward the carpool line. She said something to Andres and then started gesturing wildly toward me. I'm assuming she was trying to introduce me to him, which shows how clueless Pri can be.

Doesn't she understand that I CANNOT meet Andres in the bus line? NOBODY meets their boyfriend in the bus line! If I meet Andres there, the probability of him being my boyfriend is, like, zero percent!

I couldn't let that happen. No. I needed to meet Andres in the *cafeteria*, where most people meet their girlfriends and boyfriends! I gave Pri a little wave, trying to make it look like I thought she was just saying hello, and kept walking.

Pri didn't take the hint. She called my name and started making these big sweeping motions with her arms. Andres was kind of looking at me curiously. I guess he didn't know Pri well enough yet to understand that you needed to give her a three-foot arm clearance, because right then Pri had a slo-mo mo.

She thwacked Andres right in the nose! Ooof! I hoped he was okay! It was obviously the wrong time to meet him *then*. When Pri turned around to help him, I went on to look for my ride, crossing my fingers that Andres's nose didn't end up looking like Frankie Ziegler's.

Tuesday, October 2
Kitchen / Eighteen hundred hours

How to prepare for battle:

1. Thaw frozen cupcakes and cut into quarters.
2. Spear quarters with toothpicks.
3. Bake two dozen cupcakes.
4. Create a battle plan.

Battle Plan: Battle of the Cupcakes

Goal: Hostile Takeover of Cafeteria Cupcake Sales
Strategy:
1. Time: zero seven thirty hours. Meet Pri under awning in front of school to get "secret weapon." (She's still not spilling.)
2. Time: twelve hundred hours. Employ element of surprise by waiting until enemy camp is set up.
3. Charge! The two colonels flank the entrance and begin distributing ammunition.
4. General Tabbi positioned inside, prepared to feed the troops after they're hit with the awesome ammo.

My prediction: Maybelline will be waving the tablecloth of surrender before the lunch bell rings.

My room / Twenty-one hundred hours

After Kara and Pri left, I made my own little battle plan. . . .

♥ Operation Andres ♥

Goal: Friendly Takeover of Affection
Strategy:
1. Have Kara and Pri offer Andres cupcake samples.
2. Observe which flavor he takes.
3. Win him over by finding a chance to meet him in the cafeteria and offering him a delicious cupcake of his favorite flavor!

Once I finished with this battle plan, I had to admit something to myself: I have a major crush on Andres!

Wednesday, October 3
Mr. Pederson's room / Eleven thirty hours

I should've been able to predict what Pri's secret weapon was way before she met us in front of the school with a plastic bag full of something soft and fabric-y and obviously T-shirts. T-shirts with some kind of cupcake slogans printed on them, I was sure.

"We're really going to intimidate them with these!" she said, reaching into the bag.

Inwardly, I groaned. How was I going to explain to Pri that NO ONE has EVER been intimidated by a T-shirt with a cupcake on it?

As it turned out, I didn't have to, because the next second she was right in front of my face, waving the COOLEST T-shirt I'd ever seen.

All I could do was hug her.

"Awesome," said Kara, holding up the black tee with a cupcake-and-crossbones logo. "We'll present a united front in these, for sure."

Pri beamed. "So glad you like them! I texted Ma to order them from Johnny Cupcakes on Saturday, but she texted back that they wouldn't arrive until Tuesday. Hope you didn't mind waiting."

"It was worth it," I said, as we crowded in front of the mirror. We no longer looked like fund-raising girls. We were officially a force. My brain imagined us like this:

CUPCAKE ANGELS

Now, sitting here waiting for fourth period to start, I can say that the T-shirts are definitely getting attention and we're using it to our advantage, telling everyone they'll "find out soon" what it's all about.

I'm excited and scared. I'm happy and nervous. I feel like I'm gonna barf sprinkles!

Cafeteria / 12:35 p.m.

Mission accomplished! Details later. . . .

Family room / 4:31 p.m.

What an unbelievably great day!!!!! Well, it was a great day for *me*, but it looked like it was a pretty rotten day for

Chip, who came to school wearing his duct-tape belt and carrying his book with its duct-tape cover. Poor guy waited until Kara finished handing out samples, then came to our table and ordered two cupcakes from her, which he paid for with money from his duct-tape wallet. When he told her he loved our T-shirts, she said, "Hmph."

I gave him a small smile when she wasn't looking.

Anyway, other than feeling sorry for Chip, my day totally ROCKED. Three cheers for taste buds! Samples on the toothpicks are the way to go! You should have seen Maybelline's face when people started making a beeline for our cupcakes instead of hers.

We sold out! The only problem with that is that Pri and I can't get the data we need for our probability project. Tomorrow we're bringing in an extra dozen.

(Note: Andres didn't take a free sample. Kara says she'll make sure he gets one tomorrow.)

Thursday, October 4
My room / 7:59 p.m.

Success again! We figured out our three bestselling flavors (chocolate, peanut butter, and red velvet), so now we've started selling all three flavors every day. By keeping daily records, we should be able to accurately predict *how many* of each flavor to bring in every day in order to maximize sales. (All of this data will be used for our algebra probability project.)

Kara went back to making her index cards to reflect the past few days of sales.

Cupcakes 4 Catastrophes   10/4
Total Merchandise: 36 cupcakes (12 choc, 12 PB, 12 Red Velvet)
Price: $1.00 each

\# Chocolate Sold: 11
\# PB Sold: 10
\# Red Velvet Sold: 9
Total Sold: 30 ($30.00)

Total Needed: $600.00
Sales So Far: $116.00   (total of all days so far)
To Go: $484.00

Maybelline hasn't been too happy about our success. She spent the entire lunch period glaring at us. Kara said, "She looks like a python who wants to swallow all three of us whole."

"And our three dozen cupcakes for dessert," added Pri.

Well, *they* might have thought the anger in those greenish eyes was threatening, but I found it hilarious. I loved that the cupcakes made by the nerds were outselling the ones made by Miss Popularity. Nerdy chicks rule!

The only bad thing was that when I asked Kara which sample Andres tried, she said, "He's, like, the ONLY guy who didn't take a free sample. A lot of them tried to take more than one."

"Did he ignore you when you asked, or slap the sample away? I mean, how'd he act?"

"He said *No, thank you.* He was polite and all."

"Maybe you didn't offer him the right flavor. What flavor did you offer him? Did you try more than one?"

Kara looked exasperated. "I didn't pay attention. If you want to make sure he takes a sample, why don't YOU give out samples tomorrow?"

"I can't. You guys are standing right *outside* of the cafeteria entrance. I need to meet him *in* the cafeteria."

Kara shook her head like I was crazy, but I didn't let it stop me. "I NEED him to taste a cupcake!" I said. "Everyone knows the way to a man's heart is through his stomach!"

"Says who?" asked Kara.

"My grandma."

Kara rolled her eyes.

"And the granddad on *Duck Dynasty*! He's always lopping off the head of a catfish or the legs from a bullfrog or something while telling his grandsons how important it is to find a woman who can cook."

"You'd better find another way to Andres's heart," said Kara. "Given that we're not serving catfish or frog legs, and the guy doesn't seem to like cupcakes."

"Who doesn't like cupcakes?" I asked. (The answer is *no one*. DUH.)

"Some people don't like sweets," said Kara.

"Name one person who doesn't like sweets. I mean ANY sweets. Someone who has *never* wanted to go trick-or-treating. Name someone like that."

Kara looked irritated, but she was quiet for a moment.

"What if he's diabetic or something?" she said.

Oof! I mean, he *could* be diabetic. Then that would make me a jerk. A big jerk. Because it's kinda jerky to repeatedly shove delicious cupcakes in the face of someone who can't eat them.

"Okay, you have a point. He could be diabetic or have food allergies. How can we find out if he can't eat cupcakes for a medical reason?"

"You could just ask," said Kara. "But it's kinda too personal a question."

"Totally," I agreed. But I thought about it for a mo and came up with a fab idea. "I know!" I said. "After lunch tomorrow, I'll go tell Nurse Dobson that I don't feel good. Then you walk by the door of her office."

"What will that accomplish?" asked Kara.

"Nothing, I haven't gotten to that part of the plan yet. Like I was saying, you walk by her office — scream — and fall down. Act like you've broken an ankle."

"And that will help you find out about Andres because . . ."

"Because while you're out there loudly demanding her attention, I'll be quietly hacking her computer and reading Andres's medical file. It'll note whether or not he has diabetes."

(Kara x Fake Fall) + (Nurse Dobson Helping Kara)
= (Hacking Opportunity for Tabbi)

It seemed like the perfect plan to me, but at this point Kara threw back her head and laughed. Seriously. She laughed!!!

"What's so funny?" I asked.

Kara chuckled. "Really, Tabs, how many computers have you hacked? Ever?"

"Ummm . . . none. But people hack them all the time. It can't be that hard."

"Not people like you and me! Hackers have serious computer skills. There's NO WAY you'd be able to do it. But let's say for a second that you somehow miraculously managed to succeed. . . . If you got caught, you'd get expelled! And so would I!"

"And that's what you thought was funny? Us being expelled?" I said.

"Not us being expelled. You. You thinking you could hack a computer!" Kara started laughing again. Rude!

There had to be a way to find out if there were foods Andres couldn't eat! Kara found out all kinds of things about guys last year, just by watching them and taking notes.

I slapped my forehead. The obvious answer was staring me right in the face. Actually, it was still laughing hysterically, but it was about to be staring me in the face. I grabbed Kara's arm. "You could do it!" I said.

She stared at me. (See, I told you it was about to be staring me in the face.)

"Just observe him, like you did with those guys last year. You know, pay attention to what Andres brings in his lunch for the next few days. Gather information! You can do that, right?"

"Sure." Kara smiled.

"When you're done observing, make one of your charts or graphs to help us figure out if Andres has any food issues."

Kara was totally on board with that!

My prediction: Once we find out what Andres can and can't eat, I'll bake a cupcake that he can't resist!

Saturday, October 6
Dad's house / 4:15 p.m.

Dad picked me up this morning and brought me to his house, which is, like, forty miles away from my house, the house he used to live in. He lives out in the country now, where there is NOTHING to do unless you like to go on nature walks, play Scrabble with adults who know every word in the English language that begins with Q, or entertain a toddler who enjoys pulling everything out of kitchen cabinets, but not putting it all back in. I actually don't mind any of those things, but I don't like them enough to do them ALL WEEKEND LONG, which is why I usually try to come out here just for one night at a time.

It worked out perfectly this weekend because Kara invited Pri and me to spend Friday night at her house. We were in great moods because the thirty-two cupcakes we sold at lunch brought us to almost a hundred fifty dollars in sales: one-fourth of our goal!

My fave part of the night was when Pri took a shoe-box lid from her duffle bag and drew a grid on it. Then she told us to label the grid with boys' names. When we were done, she pulled a toy top from her pocket.

"This is a game to help predict who your next boyfriend will be," she said. (That got my attention!) She handed the top to Kara. "Spin it. It'll stop on the name of the right guy for you."

Kara spun it. The top stopped on Alex Brantley's name.

What a waste! She's never fully appreciated Alex B! I'll be jumping for joy if the top lands on his name when I spin it. I mean, he's the perfect Plan B if things don't work out with Andres. But Kara just frowned a little, and I saw her eyes dart over the square with Chip's name! (Yet when he sent her a text ten minutes later, she hit DELETE without reading it. Sometimes I don't understand my BFF.)

It was my turn next, so I blew on the top for good luck. Then Kara told me that people blow on dice for good luck, not tops, which probably explains why I had such bad luck when I spun it. I probably blew the good luck right off of that top! It landed on the square with James's name.

Evan	Malcolm	Phillip	Chip
Alex B	Gil	James	Josh
Alex L	Jonah Nate	Jake	Andres

I have to confess that I don't know if I'll ever find the right guy. I still haven't figured out exactly how to predict that. But there is one thing I can predict with absolute certainty: Tabbi Reddy will never **ever ever** take James Powalski back!

Pri took the top from my hand. "My turn. The good news is that I don't care where it lands; I'll take any of them!"

"Trust me, Pri," I said. "There are names on that lid that you're not going to want to be associated with."

"No, there aren't," said Pri. "I've never had a boyfriend. I want to see what it's like."

"It's not worth it," said Kara. "You'll think you're happy and then he'll betray you in the worst possible way."

Please. If you're gonna start a list about all of the rotten things people do to each other, I'm pretty sure *eating a cupcake* won't top it. I changed the subject. "Go ahead and spin, Pri."

The top twirled around the lid, bumping off of the sides, and finally came to a stop in the square labeled JONAH NATE.

Pri clapped her hands.

"You don't know Jonah Nate, do you?" I asked.

"No," said Pri. "But it looks like I'll be getting to know him soon."

Kara and I glanced at each other. "Don't count on it," said Kara. "This is a fun game, but that's all it is. You can't use a game, a fortune cookie, a cootie catcher, or anything else to predict who you're going to be with. It's more complicated than that."

I disagree! But I chose not to comment.

After that, we did the usual slumber-party stuff — painted nails, watched movies, and then crashed. Well, Kara and Pri crashed.

I lay awake in my sleeping bag, looking up at those glow-in-the-dark stars again. I couldn't help feeling a little jealous that the top landed on Alex B for Kara. *I'm* the one who's always had a crush on him!

Kara would say it didn't matter — that the top was meaningless — but I'm not so sure about that! After all, even though I know I'll never date James again, the truth is: He *used to be* my boyfriend. Maybe the top *can* tell who you date — it just can't tell whether you dated them in the past — or if you'll date them in the future!

When I was sure Kara and Pri were asleep (Kara started snoring and Pri stopped talking), I grabbed the shoe-box lid and tiptoed to the bathroom. What could it hurt to try again? If the James prediction was for the past, maybe the next spin would predict the future. I held my breath and let it twirl.

Alex Langford. Ugg. He's completely in love with The Sponge. I think my fingers slipped when I was about to let go of the top, though, so that probably didn't count. I tried again.

James. Didn't count.

I spun it again. The top headed straight for Andres's name! Then hit a wall and landed over on Evan Carlson's. Another ex!

I spun that top over and over, but it never predicted Andres as *the one*. There had to be something seriously wrong with the square his name was written in! Maybe there was a curve in the lid or something. I erased James's name from the center of the box lid and replaced it with Andres's. I spun one more time. The top finally landed on the right square!

But now it had the wrong name in it. James. ☹!

At that point the shoe-box lid found a new home: the trash can! And I went to bed with blisters forming on the thumb and forefinger of my right hand.

My prediction: The shoe-box-lid fortune-teller doesn't work!

Tuesday, October 9
Kitchen / 4:48 p.m.

Kara came over after school with a chart in her hand. "I know what kind of cupcake Andres will eat," she declared.

She spread the chart out on the kitchen table. It looked like this:

Andres's Lunch

Friday	Ham and Cheese	Doritos	Carrots	Chocolate Bar	Juice Box
Monday	Ham and Cheese	Cheetos	Apple	Yogurt	Juice Box
Tues	Ham and Cheese	Doritos	Banana	M&M's	Water

The only thing I noticed that he had the same every single day was ham and cheese.

"A meat cupcake!" I guessed.

"Gross," said Kara. "Why do you think that?"

"Because he brings meat every day. It wouldn't be all that hard to make. I'll make a meatloaf, divide it into cupcake pans, and put something like . . . mashed potatoes on for icing."

"Like I said, gross," said Kara. She shuddered. "Besides, there's already a food like that. It's called shepherd's pie."

"Well, the only thing he's had every single day is a ham-and-cheese sandwich. I guess I could make a ham-and-cheese cupcake," I said, thinking aloud. "I could throw in some eggs to hold the ham and cheese together."

"That's called quiche!" said Kara. "And who said that he's had a sandwich every day?"

I pointed to the first column.

"That says ham and cheese," said Kara. "It doesn't say anything about a sandwich. Or bread."

"You mean he just eats a slice of ham and a slice of cheese?"

"No. They're rolled together and held with a toothpick. Kinda ham-and-cheese pinwheels."

I looked at the chart again. "I give up. What flavor cupcake can he eat?"

"I think he can eat any flavor. It's what he *can't eat* that's holding him back."

"Meaning?"

"I don't think he can eat *gluten*. Notice he never brings anything made with wheat flour, like bread, cookies, or pretzels. Wheat products contain gluten. He can't eat our cupcakes because they're made with wheat. It looks like you're going to have to find another way to impress Andres."

I groaned. I'd never heard of a *kid* who couldn't eat gluten. Not being able to eat it can be a big pain! My aunt Sally can't eat gluten, so when we visit her we can never go out for pizza or anything.

But then I thought about some of the delicious things she *can* eat. I'm sure I've seen her eat gingersnaps! So there must be substitutes for wheat flour that you can use when baking.

It makes perfect sense. We'd used a substitute one time when making cupcakes. We needed brown sugar for a peanut butter cupcake recipe, but we didn't have any. We found a blog post suggesting we substitute white sugar and molasses for brown sugar. The cupcakes turned out fine!

I grabbed my iPod and searched for *gluten-free flour.* "Hey!" I said. "There are all kinds of flours besides wheat flour."

"Really?" asked Kara.

"Yep," I said. "Corn flour, rice flour, and arrowroot flour are all gluten free!"

"Where do you get something like that?" asked Kara. "I've never heard of flour that isn't just plain old flour."

I looked down at the screen. "Grocery stores like Earth Fare carry it."

"Earth Fare?"

"Earth Fare."

My prediction: I *will* find a way to bake the perfect cupcake for Andres. (Assuming I can find a way to Earth Fare.)

Wednesday, October 10
Band room / 1:44 p.m.

I knew Maybelline wasn't going to like it when we outsold her, but I didn't think she'd stoop to threats!

Toward the end of lunch, Maybelline glided over to our table with a crocodile smile on her ruby-colored lips.

"Looks like your business is doing great," she said. "Too bad it's your last day."

Pri jumped up and got right in Maybelline's face. It was pretty funny watching her back away from tiny Pri.

"It is *not* our last day!" Pri said. She was gesturing so wildly that I thought she might accidentally (or maybe accidentally on purpose) smack Maybelline's perfect face. "Our cupcakes are better than yours, and our sales prove it!"

Maybelline smirked.

"Our last day will be October twenty-sixth and not a day before," said Kara.

"You're wrong about that," said Maybelline. "Because if you set up your cupcake table tomorrow, or any other day, I'll show this to the world." She held up her cell phone.

"I hate to break it to you, but the world already knows about cell phones," I said.

Maybelline touched the screen with a plum-colored fingernail.

"I took this entertaining video at Triple Slice of you and Pizza Face," she said. "It's so priceless it'll probably go viral." She tapped the screen and an image started moving and talking.

It was me — bending over the pile of cheese, practically drooling. "I'll tell you what I see: the image of my future crush! Look at that handsome profile! He's perfect for me!"

My stomach sank.

Why does Maybelline always have to be in the wrong place at the right time? I looked over at Kara, and her face confirmed what my gut already told me. Even Pri had a hard time keeping a smile. This video made me look like a boy-crazy freak. If the world actually did see it, Pizza Face may be the LAST guy I ever had a chance to drool over. (Actually, who cares if the world sees it, as long as Andres doesn't?)

"So?" asked Maybelline, waving the phone in my face. "This is already uploaded to my Faceplace status. All I have to do is hit SHARE for it to go public. But" — she made room for a dramatic pause — "if you agree to stop selling cupcakes, I'll erase it."

"We can find another way to raise money," said Kara, touching my arm.

Pri's big eyes narrowed. "Five Corners Elementary needs this money! I say we don't back down!"

I thought about my cousin and the money needed to get her community back in shape. And more than that, I thought about my mom, who was so proud of my efforts and so happy that we were doing something to help my cousin's school. I couldn't disappoint them. There are a lot of things you can say about me. Some good and some bad. But when I know I'm right, I never, ever, ever back down.

I wasn't going to let Maybelline hold that video over my head. I grabbed the phone from Maybelline's clutches and did something I hope I won't regret for the rest of my life. I hit SHARE.

Family room / 3:26 p.m.

I told myself Maybelline couldn't hurt me too much. But by the time I got home from school, that humiliating video was all over my computer. My own "friends" were sharing it. It looked like it was gonna go viral in a way that might virtually kill me.

I mean, I don't really care what Maybelline thinks about me. I got over her last year after she stole Evan from me. But knowing those other people I thought were my friends were helping her make fun of me. Well . . . that really hurt.

Dianna Leroy shared the video!

James commented, "What a loser." I broke up with him, so maybe I deserve for him to call me that. But not in *public*, to the WORLD. It seems like you couldn't do that to someone if you EVER liked them, even a little bit.

Tears were already blurring my vision as I called Kara.

Kara: Hi, Tabs . . . um, you ought to know something. . . .

Me (sobbing)**:** I already know.

Kara: It'll blow over soon. There'll be another big new thing on Faceplace tomorrow, or the next day, and that will overshadow the Triple Slice video.

Me: Yeah, but Dianna and James . . .

Kara: I saw the comments. And I'm sure more of our friends will make them. Try not to let them get to you.

Me: It's hard. Because I really do look ridiculous in the video.

Kara: Well . . . yeah, but it's funny. It's not like you did something cruel or wrong. You just acted goofy. People won't end up holding it against you.

Me: What if Andres sees it? What if he sees it and decides he doesn't like me before I even have a chance with him?

Kara: It'll mean he's not the right guy for you. Besides, he might not even be on Faceplace.

I typed his name in the search bar. No matches! Maybe he wouldn't see it! It was a bright spot, but only a small one. Plenty of other people were seeing it right then. The video now had over thirty thumbs-ups and three shares. Ouch!

Me: I'm logging off. I can't let this get to me, and the only way to keep from obsessing about it is to ignore it.

Kara: You're right! Throw yourself into another project. Get your mind off of this.

My BFF was right. I needed to find something to do. I wasn't going to let the Triple Slice video bother me anymore!

After getting a very sweet and supportive message from Pri, I got to work. As I dumped the dry ingredients into a big stainless steel bowl, I couldn't stop thinking about my "friends" who had liked the video and my "friends" who were probably laughing at me behind my back. I tried, unsuccessfully, to push them from my mind as I added shortening and milk.

I cracked the eggs with a vengeance and threw them into the mixing bowl. They stood out bright yellow against the whiteness of the batter, but were eventually pulled under by the beaters. After a minute or so, they blended in so perfectly with the other ingredients that you'd never know they were there. I hoped Maybelline's video would do something like that. Stand out when it first entered Faceplace and my world, but later be pulled under and mixed in so it wasn't noticeable at all.

By the time the cupcakes were in the oven, I was feeling a lot better.

While they were baking, I looked up a couple of recipes for gluten-free cupcakes. I focused on the ones featuring chocolate, since we could tell from the chart Kara made that Andres likes chocolate. I found a ton of them! The most delicious-looking one was called Gluten-Free Chocolate Ganache Cupcakes. (Ganache is made with chocolate and cream and used as a super-rich icing for this recipe.)

I figured I should go ahead and try baking these today, because I desperately needed to keep my brain and my hands busy. It seemed like every time I let them idle, my hands wanted to grab my tablet and check Faceplace, and my brain wanted to get all miserable over what I saw when I did. Last time I checked, which was right after closing the oven door, fifty-two people had liked the video, five had shared it, and fourteen had written comments like *What a moron*.

I told myself that I shouldn't get upset about a stupid video when a lot of people, like Uncle Mike's neighbors, had lost their homes. Sure, it might mean I'd never get another date, but would that be so bad? Did I really need a boyfriend?

No. I didn't!

Hadn't I already proved that I'm doing fine without one?

Yes. I had!

But just in case I needed to convince myself of this later, I wrote down what I'd been thinking.

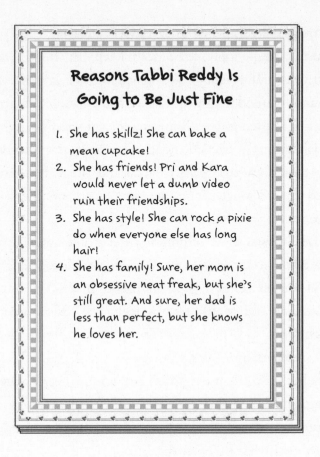

Reasons Tabbi Reddy Is Going to Be Just Fine

1. She has skillz! She can bake a mean cupcake!
2. She has friends! Pri and Kara would never let a dumb video ruin their friendships.
3. She has style! She can rock a pixie do when everyone else has long hair!
4. She has family! Sure, her mom is an obsessive neat freak, but she's still great. And sure, her dad is less than perfect, but she knows he loves her.

After reading over my list, I felt strong! I felt empowered! I felt like I could handle anything! So I opened Faceplace again.

Shouldn't have done that. Sixty-five likes and twenty-one comments! If I'd eaten an entire dozen cupcakes by myself, I wouldn't feel as sick as I do right now.

By the time Mom got home, the kitchen was spotless. I had my argument ready to convince her to run me to Earth Fare to pick up gluten-free flour.

But when I asked her about taking me, she said, "Not today, Tabitha. I'm exhausted." This is a perfectly normal thing for my mom to say, so I don't know why it had the effect on me that it did.

I completely lost it. With my pouring tear ducts and booming sobs, I was creating my own personal thunderstorm. Mom came over and held my face in her hands like she did when I was little. "What's wrong, honey?" she asked.

Somehow she managed to understand what I said even though I was sobbing so uncontrollably that it sounded like I was speaking an alien language — one that didn't include spaces between the words. She hugged me, then got up and unplugged the modem, so now I can't check Faceplace even if I want to.

"I know it hurts that your friends are laughing at you," said Mom. "But it sounds like the video is harmless. You didn't do anything wrong. This won't last."

"That's what Kara says," I sniffed. "And I've tried not to get upset when I know Uncle Mike has it so much worse."

Mom gave me a hug. "Just because something worse happens somewhere else doesn't make it less painful when something bad happens to you." She picked up her car keys. "Let's go. Mother-daughter baking is exactly what we need. You can explain about these gluten-free cupcakes on the way."

It was nice being in the kitchen with Mom again. And it felt great to share the success of the most chocolaty, moist cupcakes ever baked. I know I'm taking a huge risk trying to meet Andres tomorrow of all days — that maybe I should wait until the video attention dies down like Mom and Kara say it will. On the other hand . . . if Andres rejects the cupcakes . . . if he laughs in my face because of the video . . . then I don't need him.

I have myself, my friends, my family, and a house that smells like chocolate. What more could a girl want?

My prediction: Tabbi Reddy is going to be all right!

It started the minute the heel of my boot clicked against the sidewalk outside of my school.

"Hi, Tabbi, where's Pizza Face?"

"How's your new boyfriend, Tabbi?"

"Tabbi and Pizza Face sitting in a tree . . ."

"Hey, Tabbi, you sure have lowered your standards since your last boyfriend." The person who said this *was* my last boyfriend, James. I'll tell you what *has* lowered since dating him: my opinion of *him*.

I felt my cheeks burning. There was really nothing to do but to own it. "Maybe," I said, "but Pizza Face is a whole lot *better looking* than my last boyfriend."

LaTisha, who was walking by, looked at James and said, "Ooooooo, *burn!*"

Then James was the one with the red cheeks.

Why did that make me feel so much better? I ran my fingers through my short hair and walked away.

By the time lunch rolled around, I didn't want to spend the whole period in that room of people who'd been teasing me all day. But I *had* to make an appearance. Mom and I baked those delicious gluten-free cupcakes, and I WAS going to deliver one.

After quickly helping Kara and Pri set up the table, I grabbed a chocolate ganache cupcake and headed for the table in the right corner of the cafeteria where Andres sat. I wanted to get there before his friends joined him. Today I would meet him. It might not be the right time, but it would definitely be in the right place: the cafeteria. Right where my probability predictions indicated I was most likely to meet my next boyfriend.

Andres was tearing open a bag of Cheetos when I walked up.

"Hi," I said. "I'm Tabbi."

He looked at me. His eyes were as brown as the chocolate ganache icing on the cupcake I put next to his lunch box. "I'm Andres," he said.

"I brought you a cupcake." I smiled.

"Thanks," he said slowly. He looked at it but didn't pick it up.

"It's gluten free," I said.

I thought his dark brown eyes were gorgeous before. But when I said *gluten free*, they absolutely sparkled. Looking at them made me want to melt like a Hershey's kiss on a sun-baked sidewalk.

"Wow!" said Andres. He took a bite. And he smiled the most gorgeous smile, or I guess I should say it *would have been* gorgeous if he hadn't had chocolate stuck all in his teeth.

I know. Eww. But hey — he still looked super-cute. Believe it!

"How'd you know I can't eat gluten?" he asked. He had a slight accent . . . something about the way he said his *L*s . . . and his speech sounded, I don't know, romantic.

"Lucky guess." Obviously I couldn't tell him the truth: that I've been having a friend spy on him, take notes on what he brings for lunch, and chart it out. He'd think I was CRA-Z!

"Will Cupcakes 4 Catastrophes have these tomorrow?" he asked. I told him we would and left.

As I walked back through the tables, I'm pretty sure someone called out *Pizza Face*! But it bothered me less than before because I did it! I finally met Andres. And I met him in the perfect place: the cafeteria. And maybe, just maybe, I found a way to his heart through his stomach.

After that, I didn't want to hear the word *pizza* ever again, which meant I pretty much had to find somewhere I could be completely alone. I let Kara and Pri know I wouldn't be back, then I wandered down the hallway. I ended up bumping into Mr. Gheary.

"You're not selling cupcakes?" he asked.

"Kara and Pri are," I said.

"What flavors do you have today?"

"Chocolate, red velvet, peanut butter, and a few gluten-free chocolate ganache."

"Gluten free! You're kidding!" he said. And his big blue eyes seemed to smile.

"Nope," I said.

"Great," said Mr. G. He hurried away toward the cafeteria. "I'll pick up a few for Anna."

Anna? Did our nerdy teacher have a girlfriend? "Mr. Gheary!" I called after him. "Can I hang out in your room until you get back?"

He nodded and waved, so I spent the rest of lunch period here — alone. But it was one of those times it was kinda nice to be alone, you know? I pulled out my chart and updated it.

Boy Prediction Checklist				
	♥	Alex B	Andres	?
Party Bingo Data	Goes to My School	✓	✓	
	Met in Cafeteria	✓	✓	
	Is My Age	✓	?	
Faceplace Data (How to get his attention.)	Texting			
	Touching Arm or Hand			

I kept imagining what it would be like for Andres to hold my hand, ask for my cell number, and things like that. I couldn't stop thinking about him . . . and it was nicer to daydream in an empty room without people around to interrupt my thoughts.

Who'd have predicted I'd ever find sitting in a math classroom so perfect?

$$(Everyone\ in\ Cafeteria - Tabbi\ Reddy) + (Mr.\ G's\ Room)$$
$$= Ahhhhhh$$

Friday, October 12
Band room / 1:45 p.m.

Kara and Pri convinced me to come back to work at the Cupcakes 4 Catastrophes table today. Big mistake! I should have hung out in Mr. G's room again, or the library, or the restroom. Anywhere but the cafeteria.

The one and only good thing that happened is that Andres stopped by early for another gluten-free cupcake. And he said he'd told his mom about them. If he liked them enough to tell his mom, that's gotta be a good sign, right?

But if he witnessed what happened next, I'm not sure that's going to matter.

We were about halfway through lunch when an unwelcome customer showed up. Maybelline!

"One chocolate cupcake," she said.

Pri handed her one without smiling.

That's when it happened. Another slow-mo-mo. Maybelline raised the cupcake over her head and threw it down to the industrial tile floor.

It was like she had dropped a bomb and it blew all of the noise out of the cafeteria. And everyone, even me, was completely still. Watching. Afraid to breathe.

Maybelline's lip curled into something that resembled a smile, but wasn't. She pointed to the cupcake splatter on the floor.

"Thought I'd give you a chance to try to find a new boyfriend, Tabbi. Look closely — maybe there's a guy like Pizza Face down there."

It felt like she'd cast a spell on me. I was an ice sculpture. Laughter from somewhere was pinging off my frosty eardrums. I knew I needed to react, but I was frozen — unable to move.

Then Pri yelled something that chiseled me free. She pointed a thin finger at Maybelline. "That'll be one dollar!"

Maybelline threw back her head and laughed. And all of a sudden, it seemed like my brain kinda turned itself off — forcing me to act on instinct alone.

I was a hornet who'd met the bottom of a bare foot, a mother dog whose puppy was under attack, a hyena whose dinner was being dragged away by a lioness. I don't know if this reaction was caused by Maybelline's cupcake bomb, or by her laughing at brave Pri, but I couldn't take it.

Never in my life had I wanted to throw a pie in a face so badly. And since there weren't any pies around . . . I grabbed a cupcake, reared back my arm, and felt it suddenly clasped by the surprisingly iron grip of skinny Mr. G.

"Ladies," he said. "Come with me."

He dropped me off in his classroom and told me to wait there while he took Maybelline to Mr. O'Neal's office.

My prediction: My freedom is about to be extinguished.

Uncool Carpool / 2:50 p.m.

There is one thing, and probably ONLY one thing that Maybelline and I have in common. We agreed that we didn't have an actual fight, that no one hit anyone, and that our argument hadn't technically broken any school rules.

Of course, if I'd let that cupcake fly, it would've been a different story. So I'm grateful to Mr. G.

We weren't suspended or anything, but what happened was almost worse. Principal O'Neal put a stop to all cupcake sales in the cafeteria at lunch or any other time. It is not looking good for Cupcakes 4 Catastrophes.

And I can't imagine what's going to happen to our algebra grades. I hope we've already gathered enough information for our probability project. But I'm not *sure* we have.

My room / 8:48 p.m.

"Tabbi, how could you act like that?" asked Mom when we got home. She looked so disappointed that I thought I was going to cry. "And what am I going to tell Uncle Mike? He was so touched by your project."

A hot tear slid down my cheek. I'd let everyone down. People who'd already lost so much! How did I let a stupid girl make me throw it all away?

I grabbed a pillow from the sofa and sobbed into it.

Mom sat down next to me and rubbed my back. "When someone acts like your friend Colleen did . . ."

"Maybelline is NOT my friend!" I half cried, half screamed. I sounded like a frightened chicken.

"Well, when someone acts like her, you just have to walk away."

"I couldn't walk away; she was at MY table." My squawky voice was horrible in my ears.

Mom put her hands on my shoulders and made me look at her. "You can *always* walk away, Tabitha. If you had today, you wouldn't be forced to give up this project you worked so hard on." She sighed and pulled out her phone.

"What are you doing?" I sniffed.

"Calling Uncle Mike to give him the news. You won't get matching funds now, but it's better than nothing."

"Don't!" I cried. "Don't call him yet. Give us a chance to raise the money another way! We'll think of something!"

Mom stashed her phone and gave me a small smile. "Okay. I'll give you two days. After that I'm calling. I don't want him counting on twelve hundred dollars if we're only going to show up with two hundred eighty-four dollars."

Kara called after that to say she and Pri weren't mad at me or anything. They blamed Maybelline because "she started it." This was true and all, but what would have happened if I HAD done what Mom said and walked away? Probably then Cupcakes for Uniforms would've stopped selling, but

C4C would have been allowed to continue! How sweet would that have been?

Saturday, October 13
Family room (waiting for Dad to pick me up) / 10:30 a.m.

I know normal friends don't do things like this early on Saturdays, but I accepted that Pri isn't normal a few weeks ago. She's just Pri! So I wasn't totally surprised when I heard a knock on the door an hour ago and opened it to find Pri standing on the front steps wearing a neon-orange T-shirt with *Cupcake Queen* printed across the front. (There was a picture of a cupcake wearing a tiara on it.) Pri's face was as sunny as her shirt.

"I didn't want to wait for you to get back from your dad's to show this to you!" She handed me this chart. "Look! We have enough data to make a prediction for our probability project!"

Total Number of Chocolate, Red Velvet, and Peanut Butter Cupcakes Sold Between October 4 and October 12: 222

Cupcake Flavor	Number Sold	Percentage
Chocolate	100	45%
Red Velvet	51	23%
Peanut Butter	71	32 %

"Whew! I was afraid I'd messed that up, too," I said.

"Honestly" — Pri smiled slightly — "I was, too. But you didn't! All we have to do is take the total number of cupcakes we think we'll sell and multiply that by these percentages." She pointed to the column on the right. "That will tell us how many of each flavor to make in order to maximize sales."

"Awesome!" I was so relieved!

"The only thing is," added Pri, looking more serious than usual, "since C4C can't actually sell any more cupcakes, we don't have a way to PROVE our prediction is accurate."

Poop! We were so close to having the perfect probability project! I looked at the data again. "Hmmm. Who says we have to *sell* them to prove it?"

I had an idea. A fabulous idea. Let's just say when I shared it with Pri, she got so excited I had to duck her swinging arms.

I still didn't know how we were going to rescue Cupcakes 4 Catastrophes, but at least I can predict that our probability project will be a delicious success!

Sunday, October 14
Kitchen / 6:29 p.m.

It was actually a relief to go to Dad's yesterday since Mom was so down about the Cupcakes 4 Catastrophes catastrophe. We had plenty of cupcakes left over, so I took some along for Dad; my stepmom, Susie; and Toby. It was pretty cute watching my little brother devour the pile of icing on top! He was a sweet catastrophe, that's for sure.

Anyway, Dad asked me a lot of questions about C4C, and I told him all about the failed fund-raiser.

"How is your uncle?" asked Dad. "I always liked Mike."

It seemed pointless to tell Dad the truth about how Uncle Mike has felt about him ever since he divorced Mom, so I just said, "Fine."

Then Dad pulled out his wallet and gave me thirty dollars toward C4C!!!! Now we're up to three hundred and fourteen dollars. Over halfway to our goal!

I was still pretty depressed on the drive back on Sunday, though. My "two days" before Mom called Uncle Mike were almost gone, and we still hadn't come up with a way to raise the rest of the six hundred dollars needed for matching funds.

But then I saw a sign! And when I saw it, I suddenly knew everything was going to be okay! (This wasn't a sign like the pizza cheese head, the fortune cookie, the cootie catcher, the 8 Ball, or the shoe-box lid.) It looked like this:

Why hadn't I thought of this before? Our little town is famous for its huge fall festival! People from all over the state flock to Lakefront Park every October for delicious fried fish, hayrides, live music, and jump castles galore! We could sell a TON of cupcakes there.

I checked out the website and got all the info! Perfect!

Monday, October 15
Kitchen / 4:15 p.m.

Breaking the news to Kara and Pri about my fall festival plan did not go like I'd imagined.

"What do you mean you had to pay fifty dollars to get the booth?" Kara shouted.

"That's what it costs," I said.

"So you gave them fifty dollars of our hard-earned, already-don't-have-enough money that we might NEVER GET BACK?"

I nodded, looking from Kara to Pri. Pri's usually happy face was solemn. Kara's was angry.

"I can't believe it," said Kara. "Now we have to sell fifty more cupcakes before we can even get our fifty dollars back."

"Maybe not," said Pri. "We could always raise the price . . ."

"Yeah! We should charge two dollars per cupcake at the festival," I said.

"Two dollars?" Kara gaped at me.

"Why not? Overpaying for event food is one of the main facts of life. I mean, water even costs two dollars a bottle at events."

"You're right!" said Pri. "This will be great. The fall festival was packed last year. I bet there were thousands of people there."

I felt so grateful for my overenthusiastic friend that I wanted to hug her on the spot.

"Okay," said Kara, "I'm in. But I predict we aren't going to make our goal."

My prediction: If Kara is right *this* time, I'm not just going to hate it. I'm gonna loathe it, detest it — I'm plain old not gonna be able to take it!

Tuesday, October 16
Cafeteria / 12:30 p.m.

I was at my locker this morning when I heard it again: the *tap-tap-tap* of a foot hitting a ball. It stopped right behind me. I slowly turned around and there was Andres, soccer ball under his arm, grin on his face, dimples in his cheeks, and curls in his hair. He looked so perfect that my heart was tapping much faster than a foot on a ball.

"Hi, Tabbi," he said.

I smiled at him.

"Sorry you guys had to stop your cupcake business," he said.

"Me, too," I said. But it was kinda hard to feel sorry about anything that caused Andres to talk to me.

"Those were the best gluten-free cupcakes *ever*."

"Thanks!"

"Mind if I get your number so I can text you for the recipe sometime?"

Um. NO! I did not mind exchanging numbers with him one bit! ☺ After he walked away I turned back to my locker. I knew what I had to do. I pulled out my phone. While keeping it hidden, I sent a text.

Me: ☺

Ten minutes later I heard my phone buzz from my purse, but I had to wait until after class to check it. It was worth the wait.

Andres: ☺

Now I could check off one more box from my chart!

My room / 4:12 p.m.

Just got off of the phone with Kara. She had surprising news.

Kara: I'm back with Chip.

Me: What?

Kara: I'm back with Chip.

Me: What happened?

Kara: He did something super-sweet.

Me: As in . . .

Kara: He spent all weekend doing yard work to help us raise money for C4C.

Me: You're kidding!!!!

Kara: No. He came to my house with everything he earned in an envelope that was completely covered with duct tape. (I could tell by her voice she was smiling.) It took me forever to open it.

Me: What? You don't have scissors anymore?

Kara: Where's the fun in that? He's really sorry, you know. He didn't see our table.

Me: Yeah, I know. Someone told you that a looooong time ago.

Kara: So we can add twenty-four dollars to our total.

Me: No way!

Kara: Way!

If Chip Tyler had been in the room with me right then, *I'd* have kissed him!

Wednesday, October 17
Advisory / 11:40 a.m.

Some of the groups in algebra started presenting their probability projects today. Pri and I got lucky, though. We drew a Monday slot, which meant we'd have all afternoon Sunday to prepare.

Anyway, James and David presented today. They explained that some companies put prizes in cereal boxes to increase sales. Then customers buy multiple boxes to increase their chances of getting all available prizes. This gave me an idea for a way to ensure higher cupcake sales at the festival next weekend!

I scooted forward and whispered in Pri's ear. "We should totally do that."

She leaned her head back. "Do what?"

"Offer a prize with some of the cupcakes . . ."

But the blue eyes behind Mr. Gheary's black-framed glasses looked right at me in a way that somehow suggested I'd better stop talking.

I finished explaining after class as we walked down the hall. "We already know we're going to offer our top three flavors at the fall festival. And we already know how many of each to bring! So why not throw in a wild card . . . something we DON'T know about. Something to attract customers who have a sense of adventure. We can offer prizes with each cupcake. Something trendy that everyone will want!"

"That's a fabulous idea, Tabbi!" Pri punched the air excitedly. I took a step back. "But what can we do for a prize?"

Cafeteria / 12:01 p.m.

We just told Kara about our super-fab idea to offer a prize with the cupcakes.

She got that gleam in her eyes — the one that makes it look like she's trying to see something far, far away, like something on the former planet Pluto. "I've got it! The perfect thing. Something inspired by you, Tabs!"

"WHAT?" I couldn't imagine. . . .

Kara smiled. "Tell you what. You guys bring the cupcakes, I'll donate the prizes."

And she wouldn't say anything else. Grrrr. (And that's the grrrr of puppies playing with a sock.)

Thursday, October 18
Family room / 4:15 p.m.

On my way to sixth period, I heard footsteps behind me — the kind of footsteps that seem to be trying to catch up with someone, because they get faster and faster. The next thing I knew, ANDRES was right behind me!!!

"Wait up, Tabbi!" he called.

My feet slowed down, but my heart was racing.

When he caught up with me, he said, "I wanted to let you know why I haven't texted you for that recipe yet."

"No big deal," I said, but I HAD been wondering.

He paused and pulled something out of his notebook. It was a sketch of a girl. A very pretty girl. The drawing was . . . well . . . WOW. I was speechless. But not because the drawing was so great. Because I couldn't think of a way to ask him if this girl was his girlfriend. And I kinda didn't want to know the answer anyway.

"Selena Gomez," he said.

It took me a minute to recognize the famous face. Then I found my voice. "That's amazing!"

"Well, the drawing is the easy part," he said. "Now I have to cover it with tiny strips of paper cut from magazines." He pointed to the right corner where strips of paper were coloring the page.

"I can already tell it's going to be beautiful," I said.

"Thanks. It's my advanced art project, and it's due Monday. I'll have to wait until after that before trying to bake those chocolate ganache cupcakes. I don't know if I can wait that long to taste them again."

I had an idea. "You won't have to."

Then I told him about the extra gluten-free chocolate ganache cupcakes stowed in my freezer. I promised to bring him one tomorrow.

"Awesome!" He waved at me before turning into Mrs. Brown's class.

I can't stop smiling, thinking about Andres's brown eyes and the chocolaty good smell of those gluten-free cupcakes.

Friday, October 19
Family room / 5:00 p.m.

I boxed up one gluten-free chocolate ganache cupcake to give Mr. Gheary. I figured he'd appreciate the chance to share it with Anna, whoever she was, and I wanted to thank him for being our sponsor. I gave Andres the rest of them at lunch. When I set them down in front of him, he stopped what he was doing, which was flipping the tab of a soda can back and forth.

"Wow, Tabbi!" he said. He gestured for me to sit down across from him (eep!), so I did.

"Hold on a sec," he said. "I don't want to lose track." He went back to flipping the tab of the can. It came off after about three more flips. He held the tab between his fingers. *"H!"* He sighed.

"H?" I asked.

"Yeah." Suddenly Andres seemed embarrassed. "It's just a funny thing my sister taught me. She thinks if you say the alphabet while moving the tab back and forth, then whatever letter it comes off on is the initial of your next girl-friend's name."

I tried to keep my face calm. But my brain was think-ing . . . *Woo-hoo! He doesn't have a girlfriend!!!* Then it suddenly switched gears. *Hey — wait a minute! Your name doesn't begin with* H*!*

"Do you — uh — believe you can make predictions about

221

the future and stuff like that?" I asked. The idea that he might feel the same way I do about signs was exciting!

Andres shrugged. "Maybe. But not with the soda can thing."

"Why not?"

"Because it always breaks off at the beginning or the middle of the alphabet. I mean, if it really worked, I'd never have a chance with a girl whose name started with a *T*, for example." Andres grinned and took a bite of cupcake.

I felt the back of my neck getting warm. I didn't know what to say. . . . Honestly, I was afraid if I opened my mouth, something stupid would fall out of it. Given my track record, there was a strong probability of that happening!

The cupcake I'd boxed up for Mr. Gheary was still sitting next to me; I picked it up and stood. Then, remembering what those Faceplace surveys revealed about physical contact, I reached over and tapped his arm (That's one more box checked off!) before saying, "Gotta deliver this before the bell rings."

Saturday, October 20
Family room / 10:01 a.m.

There are so many numbers running around in my head right now that I'm feeling dazed.

Our probability project is almost due, the festival is coming up, and I'm finally making progress on my boy prediction project! I hope I can keep up with it all.

My Numbered Daze

312 Minimum number of dollars needed for C4C to get matching funds
$ $ $ $ $ $

Number of days until the probability projects are due in algebra:
2
Project Grade = X

150 Number of cupcakes we need to sell at the fall festival

1 Number of boxes left on my Boy Prediction Chart that still need to be checked off in the ANDRES column!

9,059 Number of minutes until the fall festival begins!

Sunday, October 21
My room / 9:31 p.m.

Probability Project Due + Desire to Get an A
= Baking All Afternoon with Pri

Monday, October 22
Advisory / 12:45 p.m.

We rocked the project! It went exactly as planned. Well, almost exactly. I handed Mr. G a sealed envelope with our prediction in it while Pri went down the rows of desks with a tray of mini cupcakes. Each student was asked to take a chocolate, red velvet, or peanut butter cupcake, but not to eat it.

Then we counted how many were taken of each flavor and wrote the totals on the board. Then Pri said, "Open the envelope, Mr. Gheary, and reveal the prediction!"

We were already smiling because we knew how close we'd gotten.

But before Mr. G could open the envelope, there was a knock on the door. I couldn't believe who stepped inside.

Andres!

He flashed me a grin before approaching Mr. G with a note. "My pre-algebra teacher thinks I'm ready to move up."

Andres and I have a class together. Whooopeeeee!

Mr. G took the paper from Andres and nodded. "Have a cupcake and take a seat."

Uh-oh. We didn't know Andres would be there, so we didn't bring any cupcakes he could eat.

"Wait!" I said. I grabbed the envelope, scribbled on it, and handed it back to my teacher.

And one student will not take a cupcake at all!

Pri approached Andres with the tray of cupcakes. "No, thanks," he said.

"A kid turning down a cupcake?" said Mr. G. "Bet you didn't predict that!" .

"Yes, I did," I said. "Look at the envelope." Then Andres WINKED at MEEEEEEEEEEEEEEEEE!

Mr. Gheary gave us our grade at the end of class. And I can now say that at least one of my predictions has been correct!

Tabbi Reddy and Priyanka Gupta

We used research to predict how many of each flavor cupcake will be chosen by our class of 25.

Our predictions:

Chocolate: 11 (approximately 45%)

Red Velvet: 6 (approximately 23%)

Peanut Butter: 8 (approximately 32%)

A+
(+1 student who refuses cupcake, correctly predicted, but changes percentages slightly.) Great job, girls! The prediction you put on the board is 91% accurate!

Tuesday, October 23
Advisory / 12:51 p.m.

So Andres picked a seat near me in algebra! That's a good sign. A great sign. A FANTASTIC sign! And when we were talking about why he switched from pre-algebra to algebra, he said, "When my family moved here from Colombia, they held me back so I could get used to speaking English. But now I don't need to be held back anymore, so they're trying to get me caught up with kids my own age."

Did you catch that? He's MY AGE!!!!!! Which means he's a guy who is my age, who goes to my school, who I met in the cafeteria.

My prediction: Andres will be my next boyfriend. (The probability of this is high, anyway, according to my chart!)

Boy Prediction Checklist				
♥		Alex B	Andres	?
Party Bingo Data	Goes to My School	✓	✓	
	Met in Cafeteria	✓	✓	
	Is My Age	✓	✓	
Faceplace Data (How to get his attention.)	Texting		✓	
	Touching Arm or Hand		✓	

Wednesday, October 24
My room / 8:55 p.m.

Two more days until the fall festival! I can already tell that:

Shopping for Ingredients + Baking Cupcakes
+ School = Free Time x 0

Oh! And Andres asked me if I would be there. Which means he'll be there! So now I really can't wait!

My prediction: Fall festival success!!!

Friday, October 26
My room / 10:35 p.m.

Tonight was probably the best night of my entire life. Only one thing could have made it better, and my mom basically kept that from happening. Oh. Well. Speaking of Mom, I'm feeling like I need a little space away from her right now, you know? So I came up here to write down everything that happened, because I don't want to forget a single detail. (Except for the last five minutes of the fall festival. I'd gladly forget those!)

Here's what happened:

When we got to Lakefront Park, someone had already set up a large ring of white tents. This is where vendors would be selling everything from airbrush tattoos to . . . well . . . cupcakes!

We were all wearing our Johnny Cupcakes shirts, including Mom! She'd surprised me by ordering one for herself. "I thought I should look like part of the force," she said.

My mom always looks very put together. She wears suits to work and she gets her hair done regularly. She's usually the picture of perfection. Seeing her in jeans, black cowboy boots, and a black tee was something I hadn't expected. She looked ten years younger, I swear! "You look great, Mom!" I said.

"I *feel* great, too," she said. "I don't know if it's the T-shirt or the baking, but whatever it is, it's working!" I couldn't agree more. And I was super-thankful that Mom had stepped in with the baking. She was a huge help last night and this morning. I don't know how we'd have managed to get done without her.

The October breeze was cold and snappy, so we were glad we had our black beanies and fingerless gloves on. Probably by the end of the night we'd need sweaters, too. The two hundred cupcakes (we made extra) were loaded into red wagons that we pulled behind us as we searched for the tent with our assigned number.

A vendor was already set up in the first tent we passed. Music that made me think of belly dancers played from a purple iPod, and a woman wearing lots of scarves and more makeup than Maybelline sat behind a table with a purple velvet tablecloth. A deep purple curtain embroidered with golden flames hung from a rope that was strung across the tent poles. I read the sign.

I tugged on Mom's sleeve. "I've got to do this! If she really can predict the future . . ."

"She can't," said Kara.

"You don't know that," I said.

"Yes," said Kara, "I do."

"Mom?" I asked.

Mom frowned. "As much as I appreciate the interest you have in your future . . . at the moment, you need to focus on the present. We have the whole booth to set up in the next thirty minutes."

"Okay, okay," I said, looking backward at Madame Fortuna's tent. A red-haired boy was looking at her sign, fishing around in his pocket. He pulled out a dollar and held it out to Madame Fortuna. Her long fingernails, painted with glittery purple polish, glinted as she closed her hand around the cash. Her other hand reached up and swiped the curtain closed. All I could see at that point were embroidered golden flames dancing across the indigo background. It looked like a campfire against a perfect night sky. Mysterious!

I *had* to have my chance behind that curtain! After all, if you really want your future predicted, you need to put yourself in the hands of a professional. This might be the only way to find out how Andres feels about me!

Despite Mom's refusal to let me peer into my future right then, she was in an unbelievably great mood, probably due to the fact that everyone was telling her how young she looked. I took advantage of this. "If we get set up quickly, can I come back?" I asked hopefully. "Pleeeeaaaaaase."

Mom rolled her eyes but smiled. "Only if EVERYTHING is set up in time."

"No problem!" I cheered. I practically ran to our designated tent, pulling my wagon behind me.

"Slow down!" called Kara. "You'll mess up the icing!"

I didn't, though! I hung up our sign and started arranging cupcakes on the three-tiered cake stand before the others reached the tent. Within ten minutes we'd set up our table, set out the cash box, and pulled the wagons with the extra cupcakes behind the tables so that we could easily refill the cake stand as needed.

"Can I go now?" I asked.

Mom looked at Kara and Pri. "You girls don't mind staying here in the present with me while Tabbi checks out her future, do you?" They shook their heads, laughing. "Be back at five or else," said Mom.

I took off toward Madame Fortuna's tent. There were two people in line ahead of me when I got there, and the purple flame curtain was closed. I pulled my cell phone out of my pocket to check the time. I had fifteen minutes. Could Madame Fortuna tell three-point-five fortunes in fifteen minutes? Seemed unlikely. Looking ahead *through* time was bound to *take* time.

After a few minutes, I tapped the shoulder of the little girl in front of me. She looked like she was in about third grade, and her hair was so extremely curly that it made Kara's look stick straight! Some people have all the luck. When she turned around, I pointed toward the closed curtain. "How long has someone been in there?" I asked.

She shrugged. Grrrrrr. (That's the grrrrrr of a bear whose paw got stuck in a tree while trying to scoop out honey. Like that bear, I was stuck in a bad place with mouthwatering goodness almost within reach.)

Finally, the curtain whipped back and Jonah Nate stepped out, smiling. Wild. With his obsessive interest in historical wars, I thought that boy only cared about the past! I wondered why Madame Fortuna's prediction made him smile. Hopefully she didn't foresee World War III or anything.

The kid at the front of the line stepped up to Madame Fortuna's table, and *swish* . . . the curtain blocked him from view.

I checked my watch again. Four fifty-one. There was no way Madame Fortuna would finish predicting the futures of the kid in the tent, the curly-haired girl, and me before five o'clock.

I was facing a decision between not having my future revealed, or the "or else" Mom mentioned. I didn't have to be told what that "or else" stood for. If I didn't get back by five, Mom would be furious. Then I'd be stuck having to work in a small space with a furious parent. I've pretty much avoided being in small spaces with irate parents since that time in sixth grade when I "accidentally" let go of this hideous T-shirt Uncle Mike sent me for Christmas while our car was flying down Interstate 95. I love Uncle Mike and all, but you'd have to be obsessed with self-embarrassment to wear a bright pink T-shirt with *My Mom Thinks I'm Cool* printed across the chest! "Losing" that gift seemed like the only humiliation-avoiding option I had.

Little did I know, riding the rest of the way to New England with my angry mom was actually a worse consequence than wearing the T-shirt and seeing kids roll their eyes at me. It was pretty stupid of me to "lose" that thing so early in the trip, now that I think about it.

So, obviously, arriving at the tent after five o'clock was not an option. Neither was giving up on Madame Fortuna when I was soooooo close. This only left me one possibility. I hoped my calculations were correct.

$$\text{(My Hand} - \text{Cash)} + \text{(Curly-Haired Girl} + \text{Cash)}$$
$$= \text{Me Moving to the Front of the Line}$$

I tapped the curly-haired girl on the shoulder again. She turned around and frowned. "I don't know how long he's been in there."

"I wasn't going to ask that." I held up a dollar. "I have to be back at my booth in a few minutes. I'll give you this if you'll trade places with me."

I knew I had a deal when she smiled. She grabbed the dollar and jumped behind me just as the purple curtain slid back. I hurried in before she could change her mind.

By the time I reached Madame Fortuna's table, my heart was thumping wildly. I handed her a dollar. Her bracelets jangled as she reached up and whipped the curtain across its rope, blocking us from view.

"Your name?" she asked. Her voice was deep and raspy.

"Tabitha Lauryn Reddy," I said, feeling it was important to give her my whole name, since I wanted her to see my whole future.

Madame Fortuna's sparkly-fingernailed hands reached for one of the votive candles that sat in a triple row on the table behind her. She lit the candle with a long, slim lighter that looked like a giant match, then gestured to it. "Your aroma."

As flame danced against wax, the smell of cookies — or maybe even cake — wafted toward me.

"Perfect!" I said. "You knew I loved baking?"

Madame Fortuna nodded knowingly. Her earrings, which looked like cascades of tiny golden bells, jingled.

She looked into my eyes, and I know it sounds strange, but it was like I had an instant connection with her. Like she could see who I was, where I'd been, and what I wanted. I shivered. I noticed that her eyes were two different colors. One was blue as sky, the other a green blue, like the ocean.

Then Madame Fortuna pulled a REAL CRYSTAL BALL from under the table and placed it in front of her. She ran a hand over it and gazed into it.

"I see a dark-haired man in your future," she said.

I thought of Andres's black curls. "You mean a boy?" I asked.

"No boy!" she rasped. "Man!"

I tried again. By *boy*, she might think I meant someone little, like Toby. "A man my age?" I asked.

"No," said Madame Fortuna. "Not your age. Man."

Well, shoot! My dad had black hair. She was probably seeing him. How boring is that?

I tried to get more info. "How far into the future are you seeing?"

She moved her hand over the crystal ball again. "One," she said.

"One what? One hour?" I asked.

"One dollar. One look," she said. Rude!

Madame Fortuna stretched out her hand, but not to draw the curtain back like I expected. Instead, she turned her palm upward — like she thought I was actually going to put more money into it after that last lame fortune! *Proof that she knows nothing about the future*, I thought. She was still peering into the crystal ball. Her eyes flew open wide and she gasped. For the tiniest moment, I thought I saw a flicker of light dance in the ball.

Maybe that little light was my actual fortune revealing itself to her! I couldn't walk away from that! I slapped another dollar into her hand and sat back down. (She could see into the future after all. She KNEW I'd sit back down!)

"What did you see?" I asked urgently.

"Money," said Madame Fortuna. Well, that was kind of disappointing.

"How much money?" I asked.

"Enough," she said.

"Enough for what?" I asked.

"One," said Madame Fortuna, holding out her hand again. I looked at my cell phone. Four fifty-nine. I didn't have enough time or money to stay behind the purple curtain any longer.

I stood up and looked into those strange eyes. "Madame Fortuna . . . what I mostly want to know is . . . am I ever going to find him? *The one?* I mean, is there someone out there for me?"

It felt like Madame Fortuna held my gaze for a long moment. The she winked at me and gave me a tiny nod before reaching up with her jangling wrist and whipping back the curtain.

Wow! Just when I was thinking Madame Fortuna might be a con artist, she answered my most important question for free!

I rushed back to our tent and got there just in time! Mom, Pri, and Kara had their backs to me when I arrived, panting.

"What are you guys doing?" I asked. Then I busted out laughing when they turned around. All three of them were wearing furry fake mustaches! Pri's was black, like her hair, Mom's was blond, and Kara's was brown.

"How do you like the prizes?" asked Kara.

"Genius," I said. "Alex B made them so popular at Dianna's party that everyone will want one. It's like he advertised them for us for free!"

"Exactly!" said Kara.

"We'll give one 'stache per cupcake, so customers who want all three colors will have to buy three cupcakes. That should increase sales, just like you predicted!" said Pri. "Hey, do you know your future now?"

"I guess I know *something*," I said.

"Tabs," said Kara. "You don't know any more now than you did before you lost that dollar to Phillip Bernard's grandmother." (It was two dollars, but Kara didn't need to know that.)

"Phillip is related to Madame Fortuna?" I asked, impressed.

"Yeah, but he calls her Grandma. And she can't see the future."

Sometimes Kara really gets on my nerves. "Look," I said. "There have to be lots of fortune-tellers who have grandchildren. Just because you're a grandma doesn't mean you can't see the future."

"This one can't. I've seen her in Jiffy-Quick Mart wearing fuzzy pajama bottoms and a sweatshirt."

"I'm sure she looks less like a fortune-teller in her house clothes, but —"

"She was buying lottery tickets."

"So?"

"So does it LOOK like she's won the lottery?"

When she put it that way, I had to admit that if Madame Fortuna could see the future, she'd have probably hit the jackpot a long time ago. I hate it when Kara's right!

Pri interrupted by scooting between us and plopping a big empty jar on the table.

"Who knows how much we'll get this way," she said.

"Great idea!" I said.

She smiled, took a dollar from her pocket, and dropped it in. "To get things going."

We started selling cupcakes right away! Everyone loved the mustaches, and some customers definitely purchased more than one cupcake just to get another mustache. (Most of these people had pleading children with them.)

We'd been there about an hour when Andres walked up, looking super-cute in a forest-green soccer T-shirt that complemented his dark eyes. I wished there wasn't a table of cupcakes between us!

"Hi, Tabbi," he said.

I tried to think of something clever to say, but I guess I was too nervous, so I just smiled and said, "The usual?"

He nodded. "Does that come with a mustache?"

"Sure does, " I said, handing him a gluten-free chocolate ganache cupcake and a black mustache, to match his hair.

"Are you working here all evening?" he asked.

"Long as there are cupcakes," I said.

"Well, when you get done, maybe we can go on a hayride."

My heart was thumping like the bass thrumming through the loudspeakers over on the stage. I was about to tell him I'd love to, when The Vine came inching over.

She looked at the fake mustache in Andres's hand. "I've always wanted to kiss a guy with a mustache," she said, winking.

"I'm surprised she hasn't yet," Kara muttered under her breath.

"See you around, Tabbi," said Andres. He put the mustache in his pocket.

"See you," I said.

The Vine turned to leave, too, but Kara tried to stall her. "Cupcake, Gina?"

"Uh . . . no, thanks."

"Then why'd you come over here?" asked Kara.

The Vine didn't answer. She hurried after Andres. My heart sank when I saw her catch up with him and weave her arm through his. Where was Malcolm, anyway? Grrrr. (That's the territorial grrr of a lioness.)

"Don't worry," said Kara. "He likes you, not her."

"I don't know," I said. "Malcolm liked me, but then she was at the skate park, and I wasn't. . . ."

"I predict Andres ditches her within the next five minutes," said Kara.

"Hey! I thought you didn't believe in predictions," I said.

"Let's just say there's a strong probability that a boy who pockets a fake mustache as soon a mustache kiss is mentioned isn't interested in kissing the one who mentioned it."

That, at least, made me feel better.

A rush of customers kept my mind off of Andres. Everyone from school was there! I have to admit that one of the high points of my night was when Alex B bought a chocolate cupcake from us. He obviously thought Maybelline was in the bathroom or something, because when he turned to walk away and saw her standing there with her arms crossed and her eyes narrowed to slits, he almost jumped out of his skin!

After another hour or so, we were down to a single peanut

butter cupcake. (See, I knew that was the worst flavor!) When a little boy walked up and ordered "a cupcake and a mustache," Pri took his money and handed him one of each.

She turned around with the biggest smile on her face you've ever seen. In fact, you almost couldn't see her face for her smile. We'd sold out!

"Cha-ching!" she cried.

It was time for a freak-out festival (the good kind). We grabbed each other's arms and started madly jumping in circles. Meanwhile, Mom did her accountant thing and counted the cash. She waited until we finished jumping to show us the totals.

Cupcakes 4 Catastrophes

Previous sales	284.00
Donation from Jabbi's dad	30.00
Donation from Chip Tyler	24.00
Total	338.00
Cost of festival tent	- 50.00
Pre-festival total	288.00
Festival sales	400.00
Donation jar	30.35
Festival total	430.35
From Nancy Reddy	.65

Cupcakes 4 Catastrophes total:
719.00!!!!!!

One hundred nineteen dollars over our goal! We'd get the matching funds we needed, and more. We pulled Mom into a group hug.

"You girls go on," she said, beaming. "Enjoy your success! There's an hour left of the festival. I'll lock up the money."

"Are you sure?" I asked.

Right then, a tall, thin, slightly nerdy-looking man with nice blue eyes walked up. It took me a minute to recognize my algebra teacher without his black-rimmed glasses!

"Mr. Gheary!" Pri and I shouted.

He smiled at us. "Have any of those delicious gluten-free cupcakes left? My sister loved them."

So his *sister* was the one who was gluten free! I assumed he had a girlfriend.

"No. We sold out!" cheered Pri.

"Good job, girls," said Mr. G. Then he noticed Mom. "Who's this fourth baker?" he asked.

"Nancy Reddy," said Mom, reaching out to shake his hand. "I'm Tabbi's mom."

"No way," said Mr. Gheary. "You're too young!"

Mom actually blushed! "Well," she said, looking at us. "What are you waiting for?"

Yes, what *were* we waiting for? We had the entire festival to check out!

"What do you want to do first?" I asked Pri and Kara.

They looked at me like I was crazy. "What?" I said.

"Are you crazy?" asked Kara. (See, I knew they were look-ing at me like I was crazy!)

"What?" I asked again.

"When the cute boy you've been drooling over asks you to go on a hayride, don't you think your first priority should be to find him?" said Kara.

If I'd been holding a mirror right then, I'd have been looking at myself like I was CRA-Z! How could I have for-gotten about Andres's suggestion? I guess I was still in shock by Mr. Gheary's reaction to my mom, and her reaction to him! Mom *never* blushes.

"Cell phones out," I said. Pri and Kara whipped out their phones. "Let's split up and find that boy. Text if you see him!"

And just like that, we spread out. I should have known we'd hear from Pri first. That girl is super-fast.

Actually, she's super-fast AND super-clever. She didn't depend on ground surveillance to get the job done. Three and a half minutes after we'd parted ways, she texted me from the top of the Ferris wheel.

Pri: He's getting a snow cone

Me: Is The Vine with him?

Pri: ?

(I'd forgotten Pri doesn't know about all of the nicknames Kara and I have for people.)

Me: With girl?

Pri: No

That was all the information I needed! I made like a wheel and hit the road!

It took me a while to spot Andres in the snow cone line because he looked kind of . . . different. He'd made a stop at the temporary tattoo tent. A large airbrushed tattoo of a ship floated on his forearm. And he'd put on the fake mustache. His hair and eyebrows are so dark that the mustache actually matched them. It was kinda hilarious, it looked so real. I crossed my fingers that he hadn't put on the mustache to kiss The Vine.

"Andres?"

He turned around. "Oh, hi, Tabbi! Sell out of cupcakes?"

"We did!" I said.

"That's great! Your family is going to be so happy!"

"Yeah."

"How 'bout that hayride?" he asked.

A few minutes later, we were handing our tickets to a girl in overalls and pigtails. She pointed toward a big archway covered with harvest-gold balloons. Mums, pumpkins, and hay bales were scattered around. A photo op! A man in a straw hat took our picture.

Soon we were bouncing along the lakeshore in the back of a red pickup filled with kids and hay. The perfume of sweet hay mingled with the smell of dust as the tires bumped along the dirt road. I burrowed under the hay a bit to hide from the nipping cold air.

Every time we hit a dip, Andres and I were thrown together. Most of the other kids squealed with each bump. Not me. I just enjoyed being close to Andres and looking at the bright crescent moon and its paler reflection on the rippling waters of the lake.

I wanted the ride to go on and on, but it didn't. The truck stopped and everyone scrambled out. Everyone but me and Andres. I couldn't think of any other ride or booth that offered something better than what I was doing now: sitting shoulder to shoulder with a boy I liked.

It was getting colder by the second, though, so I dug my hands down in the hay where they'd be more protected. The only part of me that was warm was my upper right arm, which was pressed against Andres's. His hand found mine in the hay. They'd have to use a pitchfork to throw me out with the hay bales if they wanted to get rid of me after that!

"That was fun, wasn't it?" he asked.

I nodded and looked up at the stars. I focused on one that seemed to shine brighter than the others. It stood out in its own little space in space. I couldn't help it. I closed my eyes and made a wish.

When I opened them again, Andres's face was closer to mine. He wasn't looking at the stars. His big brown eyes seemed focused on my lips. And because my heart understood what he was about to do, it started pounding madly — thundering like applauding hands after the world's greatest show. I leaned forward slightly, then sat up with a jolt when a squeaky voice said, "Ewwwww. There's people kissing in here!"

Andres and I whipped apart. Four little kids were frozen at the tailgate, gaping at us like we were ghosts. I wanted to scream, *Thanks to you, there hasn't been any kissing yet! Go away!* Andres winked at me, and pulled me by the hand. We scrambled over the side of the truck and dashed into the crowd.

We stopped in front of the snow cone booth. "I never did get that snow cone," he said.

"How can you even think about a snow cone?" I asked, shivering. I wasn't alone in feeling this way. The cold wind seemed to have blown the long line of customers away.

Andres grinned and ordered a blue raspberry cone.

"Coming right up, sir!" said the kid running the booth.

"Sir?" said Andres.

I giggled and pointed to his upper lip. "Oh! I forgot I was wearing it!" His tan face actually turned red. Then he put his arm around my shoulders, but unfortunately, that only lasted for about a second, because the next thing we heard was:

"You, sir! Step away from my daughter!"

Uh-oh. Mom definitely had the wrong idea. And I had never, ever, ever, heard her sound more dangerous.

Speaking of dangerous, she's stomping up the stairs right now.

Well, that went a lot better than I thought it would!

Mom even apologized, kinda. She said, "I'm sorry if you think I overreacted, but when I saw you with a man who had a mustache and a tattoo . . . For a second, I thought he was *much* older. It scared me, Tabbi."

So, an actual *I'm sorry* is way better than *I'm sorry if you think*, but hey, I'll take it.

I'm sorry > I'm sorry if you think

All in all, everything's okay. Except for one thing. Mom was in full-on crazy mode when she yanked me away from Andres. I think it kind of freaked him out, because he ripped off the mustache, said "Sorry!" and disappeared into the crowd.

I've tried texting him to explain that Mom was cool as soon as she realized her mistake, but he's not answering. I guess I'll have to wait until Monday to talk to him!!! That's assuming he'll even speak to me on Monday. What if he thinks I'm genetically predisposed to be a raving, crazy woman like my mom? He might dump me now so he won't have to deal with me later. ☹ This is torture!!!!

*Note to future self: No freak-out festivals (the bad kind) in front of daughter's friends.

Sunday, October 28
My room/ 9:00 p.m.

Longest. Day. Of. My. Life.

Monday, October 29
Uncool Carpool / 3:00 p.m.

☺ YAY! ☺ Andres was waiting for me when I got to school. And he still likes me! He was mostly concerned that I'd gotten in trouble. He lost his cell phone at the fall festival, and he's been afraid *I* didn't like *him* anymore! Like that's possible.

He sat with Kara, Pri, Chip, and me at lunch. No more rolling along as a third wheel for me! And maybe not for Pri, either. You know that Ferris wheel ride she took in order to try to find Andres for me? Well, she ended up sitting next to Jonah Nate. Maybe that shoe-box lid was a good predictor after all.

I wish Andres hadn't looked so nervous when I told him Mom wanted him to come over for dinner Friday night, not that I blame him after his last meeting with her.

Thursday, November 1
Family room / 4:15 p.m.

Mom took the Cupcakes 4 Catastrophes cash to the bank and got a cashier's check for it. Then she made a photocopy of that to turn in at her office. They matched what we earned. All of it! So now we have TWO checks for *seven hundred nineteen* each made out to Five Corners Elementary School!

Pri and Kara are coming over tonight because Uncle Mike wanted to meet the "cupcake girls" who helped raise the money. We're going to virtually present Uncle Mike and his family with the checks via Skype. (Then pop them in tomorrow's mail.)

My room / 9:01 p.m.

We gathered around the laptop in the family room right at seven. Uncle Mike was already waiting for us.

"Mike!" said Mom. I waited for her to say something else. When she didn't, I turned and looked at her. Her hands were over her mouth, and there were tears in her red eyes. I guess it is one thing to know your family is okay, but another thing entirely to *see* that they're okay. I was going to have to take charge.

"Hi, Uncle Mike!" I said. "I want you to meet my friends."

"The cupcake girls!" his deep voice boomed.

Kara and Pri were all smiles. "This is Kara," I said, pointing to her. "And this is Pri."

"We have something for you, sir," said Pri. "This!" She held up the cashier's check for seven hundred nineteen dollars.

"And this!" said Kara, holding the matching funds check.

When they moved their hands down from the screen, it looked like Uncle Mike was the one about to cry. "Thanks so much," he said. "Maddie's school really needs it."

Then he pulled my cousin Maddie in front of him, I think partly to hide his face. But she's so cute, we had a great time talking to her about noisy hurricanes; the shelter, where she made friends; and going to school in a building that isn't your old school. Aunt Sally eventually sent her off to bed and she, Mom, and Uncle Mike had a long conversation.

They were still talking when Pri's mom pulled into the driveway to pick up Kara and Pri.

I hugged them good-bye. "Thanks," I said. "I couldn't have done this without you."

"You're welcome, Tabs," said Pri. Then her quick hands flew to her mouth. "I mean Tabbi," she said. "Sorry."

"Yeah," I said. "*Tabs* is kind of a best-friend name."

"I know. I know," said Pri.

"Which is why you can call me Tabs any time!" I said.

Sheesh. Then Pri had tears in her eyes!

After a high fifteen, my two best friends went home.

Friday, November 2
My room / 8:30 p.m.

You know how I said last Friday was the best night of my life? Well forget about that. Tonight was better. It wasn't as exciting, that's for sure. It was good. Just good. And sometimes:

Good > Exciting

Andres came over for dinner, and it went pretty well. Mom only asked him one or two questions that he could have, quite fairly, answered, *None of your beeswax.*

I mean, why does she need to know how many girlfriends he's had in the past?

Anyway, he was a good sport about it. He totally charmed her by complimenting her on the chicken-and-rice casserole (gluten free). Then we had a surprise visitor: Mr. Gheary!

He said he was walking around the neighborhood and thought he'd stop in to get the recipe for the chocolate ganache cupcakes to give his sister. But his big blue eyes were looking at my mom in a way that said he was stopping by because he wanted to see her again.

"Um . . . Tabbi, why don't you and Andres go sit on the porch swing for a few minutes?" suggested Mom.

I was so shocked that Andres had to lead me away. It wasn't until much later that I realized I probably owed Mr.

G a big old favor. There's NO WAY Mom would've left me alone with Andres if Mr. G hadn't dropped by.

When we got on the porch, I had my own personal freak-out festival. The bad kind. My teacher and my mom? Yuck! I kinda stumbled around, grabbing my heart and gasping until Andres took my hand and pulled me to the swing.

"Tabbi, you know you're crazy, right?" he said.

"Why do you say that?"

"Because you act so goofy about Mr. Gheary."

"It wasn't THAT goofy," I said. "I've acted goofier before."

"I know," he said.

Wait. What did that mean? "*What* do you know?" I asked.

"I know you've acted crazier. I saw the —"

"Nooooo," I gasped. "You saw the Triple Slice Pizza video? And you still like me?"

"Of course," said Andres. He pulled out his phone and touched the screen. A picture of Pizza Face appeared. Andres held the image of the pizza next to his cheek. "I think we look alike, don't you?"

After we stopped laughing (that took a while, BTW), I told him about the cootie catcher, the fortune cookies, and even the shoe-box-lid-and-top game. We laughed some more.

I glanced through the window into our house. Mom and Mr. G were in the kitchen. She was pulling out the mixer! Were they seriously going to bake cupcakes? I guessed they'd be in there a while.

"I can't believe you thought you could predict the future," Andres said. (Now that I think about it, it is kinda funny. But I'm not going to tell *him* that.)

"Oh, I KNOW I can," I said.

"Prove it!" He put his arm around me and pulled me a little closer to him. I looked up at the twinkling stars. I knew I could make a wish. But I didn't think I needed to now.

"I predict" — I stopped for a dramatic pause — "that I'm about to be kissed."

Andres looked at me and smiled. "I'd say the probability of that happening is about one hundred percent."

Tabbi + Andres = ♥

Sunday, November 4
My room / 8:30 p.m.

Shocker! Mom actually said Kara and Pri could spend the night. And she said we could stay up extra-late, which to Mom, means eleven thirty, but I'll take it. For once we stayed out of the kitchen entirely, and we're doing absolutely nothing but sitting around in our pajamas. (Pri's are purple with tiny cupcakes on them.)

I'd already told them about the porch kiss. "See!" I said. "Proof that you should believe in predictions! The Party

254

Bingo data I collected said I'd meet someone at school, my age, in the cafeteria. And it turns out Andres is in all three categories!"

"Hmmmmm," said Pri.

"And I haven't told you this yet, but I think Madame Fortuna's prediction was accurate, too. She saw a dark man in my future. Because of the fake tattoo and mustache, Madame Fortuna probably mistook Andres for a man, like Mom did."

"Hmmmmmm," said Kara.

"And that fortune cookie said a man would walk through the golden doorway of my life! Andres walked through the harvest-gold balloon arch with me. An arch is a doorway!"

"Tabs," said Kara. She forced a big old dramatic pause on me. "Those things didn't happen because they were predicted. They happened because you were *proactive*."

Not again! "What are you *talking* about?"

"You could have easily met Andres at the bus stop," said Pri. "But you *chose* to meet him in the cafeteria."

True, but . . .

"And you researched what Andres ate and made him a special cupcake — that's taking matters into your own hands," said Kara.

True, but . . .

"And you sought Andres out for the hayride, which was through the balloon arches," said Pri.

True, but . . .

"All of that proves you were proactive!" said Kara.

Oh. Well. Maybe she's right. (I HATE it when Kara's right!)

I put my arms around my friends' shoulders. Who cares if they don't believe in predictions? I'm absolutely positive that my next one is going to come true.

My prediction: Kara, Pri, and I are going to be friends for a long, long time.

Acknowledgements:

The older I get, the more I appreciate my family, so I would like to thank my children, parents, siblings, cousins, in-laws, aunts and uncles, nieces and nephews, all of whom make my life easier by simply being part of the giant support network that keeps me going. This book owes a particular debt to my husband Shannon, who helped me create the graphic images, and who allowed me to bounce countless crazy ideas off of him. Again. I don't think I'd be the writer I am without Sudipta Bardhan-Quallen, whose friendship ensures that I don't have to navigate through the publication journey alone, despite the fact that I live at the edge of the universe. Thank you, thank you, to my agent, Rosemary Stimola, for connecting with Kara's story and helping her make it into a second book! I'm very grateful to the team at Scholastic, especially Whitney Lyle, whose flair for design has brought me another fantastic cover. Finally, I'm convinced that I have the most helpful, positive, visionary editor on the planet. Aimee Friedman, I couldn't appreciate you more.

About the Author

Kami Kinard enjoys writing about the boyfriend quest more than she enjoyed experiencing it. Her poetry, articles, and stories have appeared in some of the world's best children's magazines. Many of the characters you met in this book appeared in *The Boy Project: Notes and Observations of Kara McAllister,* Kami's first book. She writes from Beaufort, South Carolina, where she lives with her husband and two children. Please visit her online at www.kamikinard.com.

DON'T MISS:
THE Boy PROJECT

(Notes and Observations of Kara McAllister)

Another hilarious tale of middle-school boys, girls, friendships, crushes, and surprising discoveries!

$♀ + ♂ =$ ♥

I, Kara McAllister, have just had my best idea yet: The Boy Project. These charts, graphs, and observations are sure to help me uncover the mysteries of boys. Right?